D0771759

My Bird

Middle East Literature in Translation
Michael Beard *and* Adnan Haydar, *Series Editors*

English translation copyright © 2009 by Syracuse University Press
Syracuse, NY 13244-5160

First English language paperback edition 2019
19 20 21 22 23 24   6 5 4 3 2 1

Authorized translation of *My Bird (Parandehye man)*, by Fariba Vafi , from the
Persian language edition, copyright © 2002 by Nashr-e-Markaz Publishing
Company, Tehran, Iran. Permission is gratefully acknowledged.

∞The paper used in this publication meets the minimum requirements
of the American National Standard for Information Sciences—Permanence
of Paper for Printed Library Materials, ANSI Z39.48-1992.

For a listing of books published and distributed by Syracuse University Press,
visit www.SyracuseUniversityPress.syr.edu.

ISBN: 978-0-8156-0795-3 (paperback)
ISBN: 978-0-8156-0944-5 (hardcover)
ISBN: 978-0-8156-5141-3 (e-book)

Library of Congress has catologed the hardcover as follows:
Vafi , Fariba.
[Parandah-'i man. English]
My bird / Fariba Vafi ; translated from the Persian by Mahnaz Kousha and
Nasrin Jewell ; with an afterword by Farzaneh Milani. — 1st English language ed.
p. cm. — (Middle East literature in translation)
ISBN 978-0-8156-0944-5 (cloth : alk. paper)
I. Kousha, Mahnaz. II. Jewell, Nasrin. III. Title.
PK6561.V25P3713 2009
891'.5534—dc22   2009029587

Manufactured in the United States of America

My Bird

FARIBA VAFI

Translated from the Persian by
MAHNAZ KOUSHA
and NASRIN JEWELL

With an Afterword by Farzaneh Milani

SYRACUSE UNIVERSITY PRESS

First English language paperback edition 2019
19 20 21 22 23 24   6 5 4 3 2 1

Authorized translation of *My Bird (Parandehye man)*, by Fariba Vafi , from the
Persian language edition, copyright © 2002 by Nashr-e-Markaz Publishing
Company, Tehran, Iran. Permission is gratefully acknowledged.

∞The paper used in this publication meets the minimum requirements
of the American National Standard for Information Sciences—Permanence
of Paper for Printed Library Materials, ANSI Z39.48-1992.

For a listing of books published and distributed by Syracuse University Press,
visit www.SyracuseUniversityPress.syr.edu.

ISBN: 978-0-8156-0795-3 (paperback)
ISBN: 978-0-8156-0944-5 (hardcover)
ISBN: 978-0-8156-5141-3 (e-book)

Library of Congress has catologed the hardcover as follows:
Vafi , Fariba.
[Parandah-'i man. English]
My bird / Fariba Vafi ; translated from the Persian by Mahnaz Kousha and
Nasrin Jewell ; with an afterword by Farzaneh Milani. — 1st English language ed.
p. cm. — (Middle East literature in translation)
ISBN 978-0-8156-0944-5 (cloth : alk. paper)
I. Kousha, Mahnaz. II. Jewell, Nasrin. III. Title.
PK6561.V25P3713 2009
891'.5534—dc22 2009029587

Manufactured in the United States of America

Contents

My Bird

1

This is Communist China. I have never visited China, but I think it must be like our neighborhood. No, in reality our neighborhood is like China: full of people.

They say you can't see any animals in the streets of China. Anywhere you look, you see only people. That's why our neighborhood is a little different from China because we have a stray cat that sits on the ledge of the balcony, and I think the third-floor neighbor keeps parrots. We also have a bird store down the street.

When we first moved to this house, I was determined to love it. Had I not made this decision, I would have never experienced this feeling. It was very noisy. The first day, to get us familiar with the neighborhood, Mr. Hashemi whipped his fourteen-year-old daughter. Curses in mixed languages poured out of his mouth like the pebbles in our backyard.

Maman says our neighborhood is like an attic: "You can find anything there!" She is right. Our street is full of riches, several bakeries and numerous grocery stores. So many that at first I was wondering which one to shop at, so as not to insult the others. There are many fruit and vegetable markets, enough for everybody!

But the sidewalks seriously dampen my love. They are so narrow and cramped that two people can't walk side by side.

You either have to walk ahead or behind. If you look down, you see spots. The pavement is full of spots, water spots, spit, oil, or crushed vegetables that are good for psychology students who like to read people's minds.

Look around and you think it's impossible to be proud of this scene, even with patience and understanding. Smoky rooftops and laundry that seems to be hung unwashed, tall and short buildings, very close to each other. Each alley has a number of unfinished buildings, and you can see beams, bags of cement, wheelbarrows, and trucks carrying dirt.

The old homes are being taken down everywhere and new buildings are going up. The rose and jasmine bushes in the old demolished homes are so dusty that they wouldn't even inspire poets. Here and there, new homes appear a little further back than the old ones, with small balconies and latticed iron doors. The neighborhood has become like a gigolo who wears sunglasses and slicks his hair back, but his shoes are always old and torn.

The first week I discovered the park down the street, a park with more people than trees. The elders of the neighborhood sit on the benches, lined up, as if they are handpicked for public display, and placed in a show window with no glass.

When we go to the park, a triangular space at the corner of the street, the kids run to the swings and the slides at the end of the park. The park looks like hell because it is so dusty and crowded.

Amir and I walk around and predict each other's future. I always choose the best-looking old man. I don't want to pick an old, bald, ugly man and say this is your future. My old man is not so bent over that he can't see the treetops. Although his shoulders are frail, you can see sparkles of affection and curiosity through his thick glasses. But Amir picks a woman that looks like a crumpled old envelope and says, "That's you in twenty years."

When we get to the main street, the first one after our alley, I think it's more like India; a land saturated with aromas that fill the space between people. The aromas change with each breath. The smells get mixed, and my nose loses its ability to differentiate them for a few seconds. Passing the dairy store, I call out to Shahin. At the same time, I realize that my nostrils are throbbing from the overload. At that moment, distinguishing between the smell of boiled milk and cooked tripe becomes as important as the difference between a common stomachache and an ulcer.

This place, whether India or China, is full of people, most of them children. There are so many kids! Amir says there are more drug addicts than kids. A little after lunch, the alley becomes crowded. Even the parking lot becomes jam-packed, the staircases too. On a notice on the staircase, the tenants are asked not to send the kids out into the alley during the afternoon nap hours.

The building supervisor says, "Every month we post a new announcement, which is immediately torn off."

He laughs. He, himself, has three kids.

2

Our house is fifty square meters. It's the same size as a flower garden in an average house in the northern part of the city. That's why Amir says, "Don't keep saying, 'My house, my house.'"

This is the ninth house we have moved into, and we have a feeling that we never had in any of our previous homes. Amir is ashamed of feeling this way, let alone talking about it.

But I want to talk about our house because we are not the tenants of any landlords. Landlords are not evil, but they can possess your soul just the same!

Now we are free to move our furniture around without being afraid of banging the walls. The kids are free to talk out loud, play, scream, and even run. I can quit the poor person's habit of constantly hushing the kids.

I feel a sense of freedom and talk about it, but Amir does not allow such an important word to be used for such a petty, ordinary feeling. Freedom has significance on a global level, and in a historical context, but in a shabby, fifty-square-meter house in a crowded neighborhood, in a third world country . . . oh my! How can I be so dumb?

As long as Amir is at home, I am not allowed to be ignorant, so I wait for him to leave.

The backyard is full of the smell of fenugreek. The upstairs neighbor has a grinder for chopping greens, and he chops kilos and kilos of them. It took several weeks to get used to this aroma. The curtains got used to it before I did; instead of cloth, they smell like fenugreek.

I sit on the kitchen chair and look at the backyard that is never quiet and is always full of smells, sounds, and mosquitoes. The walls are cement, with three identical windows above the glass kitchen door. Too bad the sky is so far away. The back of your neck gets wrinkled if you try to see a little bit of the sky. We have done many things to make the backyard look pretty. I have installed a small aluminum awning and mounted a fluorescent light above the glass door. I have put a few flower pots here and there, and the kids have hung many odds and ends on the walls.

I have to get up and turn the lights on. Light is distributed unevenly in this house. It is already night in the kitchen. But it is afternoon in the living room and daytime in the bedroom. I call Shadi and Shahin. Where did they disappear to? After the first few weeks of being beaten up and feeling like outsiders, now they can't stay inside. With them gone, it feels like all the sounds are gone. It is rare to have no sound in the house at this time of the afternoon. This kind of solitude is not what I long for every day. This is more like having nobody! As if they have all gone and left me behind.

I cross my legs and stare at the cement wall of the backyard. I can't stop thinking about the continuation of the wall, and the windows that only give off food aromas. What is the use of looking at the wall for so long? It is better to turn my chair. Sometimes even moving the chair a little bit makes you feel better.

At this moment, I hear a sound. The difference between this house and the previous ones is that the walls don't transfer cold or dampness. They transmit sound. None of the walls are real. They are only a layer of plaster, storing sounds from other lives only to release it at the right moment. Here you don't need to put your ear to the wall. Even from far away you can hear sounds, low and soft.

But this sound is not like any other sound from this life. It comes from another world, from that distant portion of the sky. It is like a heartbeat. It is not a tape recording. It is a live sound like a tambour. Someone is playing a tambour. This building and a tambour! The sound is getting stronger, louder than all the other sounds.

I grow fast, like an embryo that takes shape in a movie being fast forwarded. I grow and I am pulled away from the chair. The backyard has come to life. The walls have moved back. The sound of the tambour comes from the fourth-floor window. Moving my hands, I flounce and twirl, looking at the window that now looks different from all the others.

I close my eyes and listen to my own heartbeat. When I open my eyes, I see Shadi and Shahin standing in the middle of the kitchen, staring at me with their mouths hanging open.

3

 Amir says, "I am selling the house."

I don't like surprise announcements. I always need to be prepared. I can't do anything unexpectedly.

That is why I am always a little behind. I am late for weddings and funeral ceremonies. Maman says, "What is the use of henna after the wedding is over?" Amir says, "The person who ignores the warning signs has to digest everything all at once." Now I have indigestion. I didn't expect Amir's announcement.

This is the first time he has talked about selling the house since we moved here. Selling means leaving, but we just bought this house—it hasn't even been a year!

Everybody is in the parking lot. To help us get acquainted, the man who is going to be the building manager asks us to say if we are owners or renters. When it is my turn, I say, "Owner." And I am surprised how sweet it tastes. I go upstairs and relish the taste like a piece of chocolate that fills your mouth with a burst of caramel. Owner! Oh Lord! I am an owner. An owner!

This word has made me feel important. I am not miserable any more. I am not without a home any longer. These walls are ours. The staircase is ours too. This bathroom and the shower are ours. The magic of this one word stays with me for quite a long time. I can't believe one word could do this to a person. I never knew ownership could be so exhilarating.

"Do you hear what I am saying? I am going to sell the house. I need the money. The real estate agent will come to see the house some day soon."

One of the benefits of getting older is that I don't get thrown into a frenzy right away. I take a few seconds and choose from possible responses. There is no need to get up and scream. I can protect the house while seated.

"You will not sell the house."

I like the sound of my voice. It is neither shaky nor worried. It is confident.

4

I go. He goes. We go. "To go" is the only verb that Amir is constantly conjugating.

Damn this luck! We have not quite had a taste of staying in one place, and he is thinking about going again.

Shahla says, "Amir's elephant is dreaming of India again."

I say, "His is not an elephant. It is a rhinoceros. The rhinoceros always goes alone. I wish I also had an elephant that was dreaming of India or some place closer."

Amir is moving toward the future. He loves the future. He dislikes the past. Especially a girlish past that does not include climbing the walls, riding a bicycle, or neighborhood kids playing soccer, a past full of whispers, gossip, and women's games, a past that ends in dark basements and closets. Amir is not willing to take even one step back with me.

I don't like the past either. It is sad because the past likes me! Sometimes it climbs up on my back like a monster, with no intention of ever climbing down. I thought that after marrying Amir I could knock the monster down. I wished getting rid of it were as easy as losing my virginity.

One night, one of those nights that fantasy overpowers reality and sincerity rules, I told Amir about the creature hanging onto my back. I felt like a hunchback that wanted to reveal the secret of her hump. Amir interrupted my ramblings. Have I loved anybody before him? He got his answer and lay down like a happy man. But I was not finished yet. I was still talking when, half asleep, he covered my mouth with his hand.

"It is not important who the others were, and what they did. Only you are important, and from now on you are mine."

His gesture was charming, but behind his loving tone there was a hint of boredom. I realized that he would not go anywhere with me. I was shocked; loneliness and dismay filled the space between Amir and me like a second wife. Many days had to pass for us in order to leave each other alone and to conjugate the verb "to go" separately for ourselves.

5

"The man was stabbing himself when we arrived. By the time people stopped him, he had disfigured himself." Hosseini and I arrived before any others. They were taking his wife away in an ambulance and saying, "She is finished."

Amir has brought news again. Father also would always come home with his hands full, with an armful of fruit. Every afternoon, we kids would wait by the door and run to him as soon as we saw him, to take the bags of fruit from him.

Maman says, "With all his faults, your father had one good habit; he never came home empty-handed." Amir does not come home empty-handed either; he brings a bag full of news, events, and stories. Through all these years, he has learned which story to tell first and which one last. He has learned to tell the story halfway and make me beg for the rest. He knows which one to tell in detail and which one to pass over quickly. He knows that I am a good consumer for all the stuff he has in his bag. Emptying it out has its own ritual. The water should be hot, the tea freshly brewed, and a plate ready full of pistachios and mixed nuts, which are not good for my skin but work well for warming him up to tell stories.

Amir says, "Shahrzad has had a sex change and is a man now."

Then Amir pretends he is Shahrzad. I could probably be Shahriar, but before I can put on his crown, Cradle Robber's voice echoes in the building. "Cradle Robber" is what Mrs. Hashemi calls the woman from the first floor. "Her husband is about ten years younger!"

Her baby is apparently in the business of buying and selling cars and is away from home three days a week. Then he shows up driving a high-end car. He parks in front of the door and you hear him yelling as soon as he gets in.

I look through the peephole. This gives me the joy of watching others without being seen. The neighbor across the hall does not have a peephole. That's why her door is often slightly open.

Mr. Hashemi is standing on the stairs, and by the way he shakes his head, you'd think he was the most peace-loving person on earth.

Judging by the noise, we can tell that he is pounding on the door with the palm of his hand. He screams, "I swear to the prophet and to the elders that I did not take it."

Before all the people in the building figure out what it was that he did not take, you hear Ida yelling.

The kids are asleep. I sit by Amir. His tea is getting cold, and he is not eating nuts anymore.

"I don't know what happened to Hosseini. All of a sudden he had to go home and told me to make up an excuse when the boss asked about his whereabouts."

He gets quiet.

"Shall I warm up your tea?"

He says, "Why did he go?"

I shake him gently, "Never mind. Tell me something good, something about love."

"Where is love? It's all dirty stuff. When our Canadian visas are approved, we will get rid of all this."

6

Amir is in love with Canada. Everybody knows about his passion. Anybody who hears something new about life in Canada passes the news on to him. Sometimes he talks about Canada, as if he has lived there for years. He sighs and says, "I'll go to Canada and be rid of this place."

When he hits a dead end, he says, "Canada is totally free from bad luck and problems."

Years ago, Amir was able to go from Baku to Turkey and from there to the Greek border. He has talked about that foolish risk he took at least a thousand times. He got off at a train station to get a cup of tea, only a cup of tea. But before taking a sip, he experienced one of the most important moments of his life; he felt the humid air, the store window full of colorful drinks, the green bench where he was sitting, and then a heavy hand landed on his shoulder, and the harsh voice of a Turkish policeman asked for his passport.

Years had to pass for the barbwire at the Turkish-Greek border to prick him but not hurt. "Oh, I would die for those barbwires now. If I get there ever again, I would be gone forever. I wouldn't even look back."

Shahin sighs like Amir, looking at the ceiling and gesturing like him! "I wouldn't look back either, if I went."

We both look at him.

14

"Because I don't have anything here, no bicycle, no skates, no computer, no nothing!"

Amir says, "A bicycle is not what you need. You should study; education is what you need to make a living these days. You need a skill."

Shahin wants to have a bicycle.

"I don't want you to run around in the streets. I want you to grow up."

Shahin says, "I don't want to grow up. I want a bicycle."

"You need to get a job and buy the bicycle with your own money."

Shahin does not want to work. He wants to ride a bicycle.

These kinds of things make Amir angry. He raises his hand as if he is going to slap Shahin hard. But all three of us know that his hand will not touch Shahin. Last week when Amir's hand did come down, without trying to run away, Shahin said, "When we move to Canada, you cannot hit me. I will call the police."

Shahin does not run away. He slowly gets up and goes to the backyard.

Amir starts ranting and raving, and to make up for not hitting him, he runs after Shahin. Suddenly, it starts raining. Shadi and I follow Amir. Big drops of rain beat on the aluminum awning rhythmically. The single beats of the drum get louder. I tell Shahin and Shadi to go in and do their homework. They both disappear. Amir moves away from the awning and stands in the rain. The uproar created by the rain and the drum fills the backyard.

I go inside to the kitchen and say, "Come in."

He doesn't see me. He doesn't hear me. He squats out there, clasping his hands behind his head. The cement wall behind him is covered with rain spots.

"Get up and come inside."

Where is Amir? Maybe back to the barbwire or somewhere on the other side of the world. Don't know. He is no longer in this house. He is gone.

7

I call Shadi. She doesn't answer. With all the noise coming from the parking lot, I can't hear her. I look out the window. Shadi is not there. I send Shahin to look for her. Shahin returns, holding on to her arm tightly, and tugging at her. Shadi is screaming.

"I told you to find her, not to beat her up!"

I sit Shadi in front of me and give her a little lecture—what Maman should have done with me and never did. If I wanted to say something, I would pace up and down the room seven or eight times. I felt my heart in my throat and could not talk because it seemed like my words were stuck at the bottom of a deep well.

I have to teach Shadi to be careful. Maybe someone will show kindness to her. There are a hundred types of kindness, and she should know the difference. I want to teach her to watch out for the big boys who are going in and out of the building all the time. I don't know how to tell her tactfully that someone might want to touch her body. That she should scream. Shahin asks, "Why, Maman?"

"Because it is important."

The kids look at me. I grab Shadi's doll, and squeeze her stomach. The doll cries. I say, "Like this."

17

I take the battery out of the doll and squeeze it again. I say, "See, if you don't make a sound, you are as bad as a doll without a battery, without a heart. Then it is possible to hurt you because nobody will even find out."

I hit the doll hard. Pull on her hair, and ask Shadi, "Do you understand?"

I sound too harsh. Shahin is looking at me approvingly, but Shadi bursts into tears. I caress her hair and the doll's, and end my speech.

Shadi starts talking, "Ida buys fruit roll ups and ice cream; she buys candy. But I don't have any money."

I feel like a defeated speaker who has talked about art for an hour to hear the audience ask questions about economics.

"Ida has sunglasses. She has a bicycle, but I don't have anything."

I tell Shadi that she has a lot of things too. Shahin says, "She doesn't have any brains."

Shadi says, *"You* don't have any."

Shahin has found an excuse. He is getting ready to attack. "Come on. Tell me what I don't have?"

Shadi opens up her fist and laughs. "Nothing."

8

Maman left our house without saying good-bye. She was either too sick and forgot to say good-bye, or she thought about it and ignored us on purpose. Right by the door I have hung a rectangular mirror on the wall where I could see Amir's sneering face. He doesn't like Maman, and at times like this, he even despises her. Maman knows this. I know she is leaving our house with this understanding.

Tonight Maman went to the bathroom more than ten times in an hour and wept.

"You shouldn't have mixed cream into the soup. My blood pressure has gone up."

Trembling, she pulled the blanket up to her shoulders. "If I were home, I would have brewed mint tea. Perhaps the soup didn't agree with me."

Without saying a word, I went to the kitchen and came back. But in reality I was thinking about the mint and her high blood pressure. I didn't say anything. Wondering about my silence right at that moment, it felt like noticing suddenly that I was wearing a borrowed dress.

I remembered that my silence has a history. I have been praised for it time and again. I was seven or eight years old when I realized not all children have this virtue. My silence was considered my best asset. One day Father took me to the basement and asked, "Where did you go with Aunt Mahboub yesterday?"

I went mute, not out of wisdom but out of fear. My instinct told me that the answer to a question asked in the basement without turning the lights on would bring disaster. Father looked at me suspiciously. I didn't look like a mischievous and scheming little girl at all, and since he was not a persistent person anyway, he gave up very quickly and left the basement. The reward I got from Maman's gentle tone an hour later turned my simple and cowardly act of going mute into a meaningful and wise silence.

In later years, I was repeatedly admired by the women in the family for being reserved, for being secretive. I soon realized that I was like a chest full of secrets with a tight lid.

Aunt Mahboub praised my silence, and later on others echoed her praise. If a secret was exposed, if something was revealed, all eyes would turn toward Mahin. I was immune from all suspicious looks.

It was after Father's death that I broke my silence by screaming. I was sick and tired of my assigned role. I wanted the whole world and everybody to know everything. I didn't want to be anybody's accomplice, even my mother's. That's why I screamed. Father had died lonely and like a child. This was tormenting me. Maman answered my screaming with more screaming. Shahla and Mahin took Maman's side. They said I had become foolish and I'd better shut up, but I kept screaming. Father had died like a child. His head had slipped off the mattress and he had died. Mahin had to kiss my face, begging me to leave the basement. I had never felt as close to Father as on the day he died.

Shahla said, "If you remember how mean he was, how oppressive, you'd calm down." But I kept screaming that if he was a bully, why didn't he die like one? Maman was shouting too. That morning of screaming made me feel absolutely helpless. I realized that there would be no truth exchanged between Maman and me.

When I moved from Father's house to Amir's, my secretiveness had no use. Amir was frustrated with my silence. He wanted me to talk about everyday events, about the neighborhood news, about Shahla, about Mahin. There was no room for secrecy in our new life. It would create distance and cause suspicion. If something was discovered later than it should, a fight would break out. Amir wanted everything to be transparent. My silence scared him. Slowly I got used to rambling, even when it wasn't necessary. Years later, I learned that talking can even be a better cover than silence.

But even with years of practice, my inside dialogue was never completely revealed to the outside world. I am still considered a quiet person. Maman says, "Bless his soul, you take after him. Your father would hardly say two words."

We both remembered at the same time that he did talk in his final days. "Too much talk," Maman stresses. "Nothing worthwhile."

Tonight I didn't brew mint tea for Maman even when she said, "God, my blood pressure has gone up." I didn't say, "You can take a pill." As Shahla would have said. I was busy. The fridge door was clean but I was wiping it again and consider-ing cleaning the old spots on the stove. Right then I knew I should say something no matter how irrelevant or stupid.

My silence was bothering me like a tight woolen dress in hot weather. I wanted to take it off. Maman was weep-ing while putting on her shoes, and I still couldn't play the role I expected of myself. I remained right there at the door. Maybe everything would go back to normal; a routine good-bye between mother and daughter. I needed this old world ritual that sooths the pain like a balm. But Maman disap-peared in the stairway and didn't even glance back.

9

Maman doesn't cry only when she is in pain. She cries when the phone rings a lot or the television is too loud. She cries when she is cold and can't stop her shivers with blankets, or when Shahla comes from work and goes straight to her room. When she goes to the bathroom, you can hear her wailing as if she has a burning infection. Maman cries even in her sleep.

Her wailing is not related to old age. Years ago, when Father brought company home and ordered dinner, her wailing echoed in the basement. It echoed in the rooms. It echoed in the backyard. Then Father would inevitably throw something at the wall to stop the wailing.

But the noise never stopped. Father sold the turntable and bought a radio. He turned the volume high, but the weeping didn't stop. Maman carried this noise with her like an electric device.

When Father was on the road, her weeping subsided. Our ears no longer felt like ears. They were merely soft pieces of flesh attached to the sides of our head without any specific function.

After Father became housebound, Maman's weeping escalated, as if now it was intentional. It wasn't the sound of crying. It was disgust. It was hatred. It was pain. Her weeping felt like an electric current passing through your body and drying your blood instantaneously. The noise was unrelenting, and no other noise, from Father's screaming to the sound of the water fountain in the little pool, the clinking of the soda bottles, or Aunt Mahboub's laughter, could compete with it.

Father took refuge in the basement and stayed there until the end. Maman's wailing passed through the doors, the walls, and our bodies, and continued in our dreams.

10

The problem was that Father's heart was healthy, but his legs didn't move. The brain didn't communicate properly. His speech was troubled, and he was confused. Amidst all this, his heart was like a general who continued to give useless commands in a battle that had already ended.

The first time he got lost, like all things that are good only the first time, he received everyone's attention for a few days. We told everybody the story of his getting lost, and he laughed more than anybody. But nobody felt like laughing the second time he got lost. An older man brought him home and delivered him to us in a humiliating way. His pants were wet, and he said he'd taken to the road.

In days to come, it was the longing for the road that brought him out of the half-lit basement. Shahla wrote the home address on a piece of paper and put it in his coat pocket. Father thanked her like a respectable gentleman.

He then asked for "that stick." He meant his cane. He came back and said he had forgotten to take the thing that has two lenses and is worn on the eyes. Mahin gave him his glasses. His speech was like a riddle that each one of us loved to solve first. But this habit got old pretty soon too, and the puzzles of his final days were never resolved.

11

Aunt Mahboub didn't have any children. Sometimes she needed a child in her life, and she'd borrow one of us from Maman. Shahla was too old to be a child. Perhaps she had previously played a child for Aunt Mahboub. Mahin was too much of a brat and unruly. I was more suited than anybody else.

Aunt Mahboub would give me a bath before anything. She put me between her strong legs and would wash my head as if there was nothing soft in it. She used all her might. Changing my clothes, she'd say, "Your mother is sloppy." In a few hours, I was transformed so much that I didn't know what to do with my new self. That's what she wanted. She wanted to cleanse me of my old ways and to mold me the way she liked. She taught me how to eat properly, how to give thanks in a clear voice after eating, and how to wash myself in the toilet so I wouldn't smell.

When my training was over, Aunt Mahboub would allow me to treat myself to the chocolate on the coffee table.

She said, "Think of this place as your own home."

I wanted to but I couldn't. It was not my home. Uncle Qadir, like an old doorman, was always watching with his half-open eyes. He smoked a water pipe day and night and stopped only when he wanted to confirm what Aunt Mahboub had said or to give me an unfatherly wink. As if he couldn't wink without removing the hookah from his mouth.

It wasn't only Uncle Qadir who obeyed Aunt Mahboub like a devoted servant. There were a lot of people who smiled at Aunt Mahboub's remarks sheepishly and nodded their head for no reason.

Aunt Mahboub knew how to do a lot of things, from concocting remedies and medication to telling fortunes, praying, magic, and sorcery. At the right time, she even knew how to sing and dance. Neighbors would come to visit her. Even Maman turned off her weeping machine for a few hours and looked young and happy when she visited. Aunt Mahboub would torment Uncle Qadir to the point that he'd quickly turn purple. She made him keep the hookah's tube in his mouth and not even raise his head to acknowledge her comments.

Aunt Mahboub could go anywhere, something Maman couldn't do and was always envious of. Aunt Mahboub's return from her trips was different from Father's. Father always brought all the road dust with him. He would collapse in the middle of the room asking us to spray water on his chest and to massage his arms and legs. The smell of his sweat filled the house. Maman had to wash the rags from the car and his dishes that looked like they had been used by a dog.

Aunt Mahboub brought with her the kinds of things that smelled like perfumes from unknown lands. Aunt Mahboub was generous and brave.

"Mahboub has a big heart," Maman said. "Mahboub could climb up a straight wall. Boys in the neighborhood were terrorized by her. She was never drab like me."

The first time I went to the movies with Aunt Mahboub, I watched two films at the same time; one with my entire face and the other with half my face. I didn't understand much of either. When I described the movies for Maman and Shahla, Shahla understood the one that I had watched with my entire face and Maman the one that I had seen with half my face. That evening, Aunt Mahboub sent me back home for the first time.

"I don't like tattletales." She pressed her hand on my bony chest. "A woman should learn to keep everything here. Do you understand?"

I understood.

12

I tell Amir, "I am not leaving this place."

"When I leave, you will be leaving with me, and when you come, you'll be thankful because I have saved you from this place."

His voice is gradually growing louder. As if he is addressing ten people. "Nothing improves by staying."

"Calm down." I point to the children.

He says quietly, "You'll stay here and rot. There is no future here for you, neither for you nor for the kids. Do you understand?"

I realize that today Amir is planning to do something about our future.

"You'll travel for the rest of your life. You should thank God that I am providing this opportunity for you, the possibility of traveling, experiencing life, seeing the world, living."

Amir comes closer and, as if he wants to say something private, he becomes more quiet and intimate.

"I say this for your own sake. Maybe when you are there, you won't even love me anymore. You may want to go your own way." Snapping his fingers, "You'll start a different life."

When the future is in Amir's hand, it can take any shape.

"What keeps you here? What attachment? Shahla?"

29

Amir knows that although my last name and Shahla's are the same and that Father and Maman are our parents, we have nothing in common.

Shahla is fat with a very beautiful nose. Her eyes are like hazelnuts, round and dark, and her double chin is the first thing you see. Everybody says Shahla takes after Maman. I am bony and I have inherited Father's nose, which is always the topic of conversation. "Wouldn't it be better to have plastic surgery?" I'll do it if I have the money one day. But before that day, I have to do a thousand other things with the money.

Shahla is the master of giving advice. "Before your surgery you should buy a few dresses for yourself and get rid of your clothes. They look like they're from the ancient Sassanian dynasty."

Amir says, "It's this kind of behavior that makes me call you a polar bear. You are afraid of change. You are afraid of moving. You like to stay put. You think the world remains the way you want. Anyhow, is this any good? Answer me. Is it what you want? You're so withdrawn into your own life that you have forgotten there is another way to live. This is not life you're living."

Where was I the day Amir started thinking about a different kind of life?

"Even Mahin who was your mother's one and only darling, and dependent on her, cut loose and left. But you!"

Amir knows well that I am not attached to Maman. It doesn't bother me not to see her for days. But he doesn't know that I always think about her. He doesn't know that I can't stop thinking about her. He doesn't know that Maman is like a mystery to me.

I ask her, "Tell me about Vitamin."

The orange that Maman is eating is perhaps sour enough to make her pucker. She says, surprised, "The vitamins in the orange?"

"No, Father's Vitamin."

I have caught her off guard. She knows well that I don't want to hear about lice, dandruff, and a thousand other incurable diseases. About the water that was brought from far away, and cold nights, and the fire that was impossible to start in the wood stove. She knows that I have no interest in remembering dirty baths and unpaved dusty roads, or the few and far between cars in the streets of those days.

"Bless your heart. I don't even remember what I ate yesterday. You want me to open a grave?"

I want to say that inside me the graves are still open. I haven't covered them over with dirt yet. The dead are lying with their eyes open.

Maman must talk. Otherwise, how can I find out why she didn't go downstairs that night? Why did she lie down like a corpse with her eyes wide open and remained still for hours in the dark?

Aunt Mahboub says, "I married Jafar only to be able to wear lipstick."

Jafar was her first husband.

"They said you can't wear lipstick before you get married."

Maman doesn't know why she married Father.

"One day they gave me to your Father. I thought maybe he is my second father and now I should be his daughter. Somebody punched me on the side and said, `He is not your father, he is your husband.' From then on, any time I got punched I knew something important was about to happen."

Amir says, "When I married you I told you I wanted a life partner, not an obstacle on the road."

I don't remember Amir saying anything about a road.

"I need help, support, and encouragement. Partnership. Otherwise, the world is full of prophets of doom who know how to dash your hopes."

He holds my hand and pulls me up.

"How come your belly doesn't get any smaller? Ha? I want to see you there with a new look, a new you."

He puts his arms around me and dances to an imaginary song, moving me with him here and there. "Traveling is good for your soul. We will see new people. Find new friends. We ourselves will change."

While dancing you can't ask how we are going to change or what we are going to change into. Amir turns me gently. How kind he has become. How soft his voice is. He closes his eyes. I can't do that. Somebody's eyes should remain open to keep away from the furniture, and Shahin's craft project that I didn't have time to pick up and is left on the floor. I envy Amir for being able to change his fate by closing his eyes and imagining himself in a better place.

I say, "Oh, I am sorry."

I had stepped on his toes.

13

I have seen the big building where Amir spends half of his life, and the people in it. I know their habits. I know who has kids and who doesn't, and whether the problem is with the man or the woman. I know who is a Turk and who is Isfahani, who is stingy and who is generous, who is complicated and who is naïve and simple.

Amir quotes someone and I know whose mouth those words came out of. He tells a joke, and I can guess who told that joke and who laughed the hardest.

Amir analyzes people's lives and I quietly follow him. Today, Amir is talking about Hosseini and has a new story for me.

"Hosseini's wife is cheating on him."

"Manijeh?" I choke on a sugar cube. "No, I don't believe it."

"When he believes it, who are you not to believe it?"

"He is imagining things."

"I told him the same thing. You know what he said?"

He turns off the lights.

"Well, tell me."

"The big guy turned red. Got all choked up and said he wished he was imagining things." Amir turns to me. "What do you think is the matter with Hosseini?"

"How come?"

"Well, you women must understand each other well, two beautiful daughters, a nice house, and poor Hosseini has dedicated all his life to his home and family. Then his stupid wife . . ."

I am a little bit confused. I don't say anything.

He says, "Do you know what is the first thing he does every morning? He picks up the phone and starts dialing as soon as he gets to work. I kept thinking he is calling an office or something. He does this several times in a matter of a few minutes. Today I finally figured out why the poor guy lights up a cigarette each time after he dials."

"Well?"

"Don't you get it? Well, the poor guy calls home and it's busy."

I say, "Is that all?"

"Is that not enough?"

"A busy phone does not mean anything." And I think of Manijeh, usually quiet and depressed.

"Hosseini is almost sure that the foolish woman is cheating on him."

Amir does not know that I cheat on him a hundred times a day; when his underwear is left in the middle of the room, just as he took it off. When, at a party, he is so involved that he does not notice me. When he is finished eating and realizes he didn't wait for us, when he thinks of me as the reason for his failures, when he praises another woman in front of me, when he can enjoy everything all by himself. When he leaves me alone, I cheat on him. Sometimes I get discouraged, and I repent. I return from where I was going and put my fingers through his hair. He bends his head so my fingers fall to his neck. "What is going on?"

I yell at him, "See, when I don't show affection, you ask what is going on, and when I do, again you ask the same thing."

He doesn't know that I cheat on him a hundred times a day. I leave this life a hundred times a day. Like a terrified woman who has never left home. Gently, slowly, and quietly, even though scared to death, I secretly go to places that Amir cannot even imagine. Then, in a dark night like tonight, I return home to Amir, as a regretful woman who has repented.

14

Shahin is sent to the backyard. He will come in only when he has understood that even if he does not like his sweats, he has to wear them and not run around the house naked.

Two hours have passed and Shahin has not figured out yet that he is not a prince. He is the child of a family with many limitations.

Amir leans his head against the window looking at the backyard and says, "Do I like to get up in the dark every morning and go to that dreadful place? Do I like to obey the person who is called my boss but doesn't understand a thing?" Amir has remembered again all the things he doesn't like in this life.

If only Shahin nodded in agreement, he could come in and eat dinner. But instead he hollers from out there, "I will not wear those sweats."

Amir holds up the sweats.

"Are they torn or old?"

Shahin says, "I don't like the color."

Shadi brings another pair.

Shahin yells out, "I don't like the style."

Amir holds his head. "Too bad!"

Shahin has issues with his shoes, with his shirt, with his wristwatch, with his hair.

Shadi screams, "Well, he doesn't like it. You can't force him, leave him alone."

Amir goes to the backyard, grabs Shahin by the shoulders, and picks him up.

I gently say, "Let go of him."

Shadi yells, "Leave him alone."

Amir leaves him alone and sits down at the dinner table. By now the food is cold, and nobody wants to eat.

15

I am looking for Shadi. She is not in the parking lot. I go through the narrow walkways of the storage rooms. She is leaning against the door to the last storage room, and it is very hard to see her in the dark.

"What on earth are you doing here?" I shout.

She puts her finger on her lips. "Shhh. Ida is going to find me!"

I yell, "Come on, get out!"

Her eyes widen. She steps further back. She is glued to the door. I point to the outside and tell her again to leave. My voice echoes in the hallway. Shadi is pouting and doesn't take her eyes off me. I have forgotten that I am blocking the doorway like a giant, and she can't get out.

Shadi loves hiding. She has a habit of crawling under the couches, crouching behind the bed, hiding in the linen closet. The day we moved in, she got lost among the furniture. I called her.

"Where are you hiding?"

She did not yet know her way around the house. So she said, "I don't know where I am either."

I told her to come out before she got used to those kinds of places. Before the smell of the basement gets in her head and stays there forever. I get closer to her, hold her shoulders. Why doesn't she talk? Doesn't she hear me?

She has gone mute. A muffled sound comes out of her mouth. I see the fear in her eyes. I recognize silent crying very well. Silent crying means that she cannot leave. Squatting, I hold my head in my hands. I hate for my daughter to be like me. I don't want her to be like Maman or Shahla. I don't go looking for similar traits, but others find them and readily present them to you. I don't want Shadi to take after me.

I was afraid of the dark, the basement, and the shadows, afraid of Uncle Qadir, even Maman and Aunt Mahboub. That is why I kept silent. I would do anything to go unnoticed. Little by little, I got lost in my own world, and one day, I had to ask myself who I was. I grew up with the sense of being lost, a deep sense of bewilderment, with no hope of ever being found. But what is Shadi afraid of?

She slides and passes by me very quietly. I can't move. Later, when we go upstairs, Shadi draws me with two big horns on my head and big teeth like a boar. Whenever I yell at her, she draws this picture and quietly places it in my way. For a moment, I forget why I am sitting there at this time of the day.

My bare feet tingle. I think maybe an insect has climbed in through the hole in my slippers. I jump. Shadi is close to me, touching my toes with her finger through the hole in my slippers. I bring her hand to my lips and kiss her fingers. She throws herself in my arms and cries. Ida is standing in front of our storage room and yells, "Miss Shadi! I finally found you."

16

I don't enjoy the cool air of the air conditioning because Amir has to work in the hot sun. After lunch, I don't take a nap because Amir does not have the time to do that. I don't socialize with my friends because Amir can't do it. Amir is a slave, a slave who has pre-sold his productive energy for the next twenty years. Amir owes the bank for another twenty years. The bank has bought his labor from him. It is not fair to have his face burn under the sun while my face is gleaming because of eating and sleeping well. It is not fair. Amir is looking for justice, and he can't find it anywhere. The kids are noisy. Amir says he is chained to us, to this kind of life. For how long? For the rest of his life.

Amir brings in money and we spend it. We are consumers.

I say, "I will get a job. I have worked before. I can do it."

"If you want to be useful, it is better to raise your kids well."

Shahin hits Shadi, and Shadi spits. Amir says, "See?"

He claims, "Leaving is my only option."

"You will be a slave, even if you go there."

I have given the war signal.

He sits up, "Can you please explain why?"

"Because you were born a slave. Who do you think your father was?"

He must have misinterpreted my question, because he screams, "My father was an honest, hard-working man. But your father . . . !"

He wants to talk about my father. I jump in, "So, was he a slave or a hard-working man?"

But he does not answer. He has found what he was looking for—my father.

I know my blood will get to the boiling point. Amir is persistent, and will not let go until I lose it. I can't hold it in any longer. I am forced to do it on my own.

I say, "Whatever my father was, we weren't ashamed of him."

I pause, so the next blow has a stronger impact. "Do you remember saying you would die of shame whenever your father came to your school?"

He doesn't believe that I can be so ruthless and take advantage of his heartfelt confessions. He doesn't know that I would take my strong, well-dressed father a hundred times over his disheveled father. It is too late now. We can't choose one over the other, now that they're dead.

He shakes his head. I know he is cursing himself for being so naïve. I have made his sincerity look like stupidity.

He says, "Your father was only good at one thing: seducing other people's wives."

He turns all red.

I say, "That is the basic story of all the world's exciting movies."

I realize that I am being very stupid. The fighting engine has started. Sometimes it is hopeless; the quarrel goes on and on no matter what you do. No amount of wisdom can stop it. He says one thing and I say something else. There is no joy in defending something you don't believe in. Amir puts me in this position. I don't like him. He makes me feel like an ugly witch. And why not get uglier? Amir is on a roll and does not stop. He gets excited about what he is saying. It is at a point when I have to yell.

It took me years to realize that one scream is equal to three hours of begging and pleading. Like lightning, a scream will burn everything all at once. It took me years to figure out that people unknowingly need to be yelled at. They need a loud sound to make them listen at the appropriate time, and to drown out the unwanted noises around them, to remember that there is someone else sitting in front of them. I yell. Loud and clear. Without crying or moaning. That's what Amir calls feminine deception. I know that the "Young Rooster" is behind the door, and that Mrs. Hashemi is bending halfway out of her window in the backyard.

Amir says, "Keep your voice down."

I don't. I stand up so that the sound carries better. I am glad that our house is so small that he can't run away from my screaming.

Quietly he says, "I will divorce you."

It's like a deadly bullet that he has fired calmly.

I must be dying. I lie down to die, but I don't die.

17

The basement I see in my dreams has no windows. But the basement in my father's house had windows; four small windows. The basement in Aunt Mahboub's house had only one window that could be seen from the backyard. Our basement was big and full of old furniture, kerosene barrels, and pickle jars. Coming down the stairs, first you saw the small basin in the corner and the twin trunks with packages of lavash bread on top. The basement had a low ceiling. Whenever I start traveling to my past, I end up in this basement that, through its winding passages, was also connected to Aunt Mahboub's basement.

After Father's truck accident, he bought a taxi with the rest of his money and retired. He did not know the house well, and when he became housebound, he could no longer run the house. The house became full of shadows that he brought in with him, the same shadows that came to life on the white walls when Uncle Qadir cut down the big rose bushes. The silent movements of those shadows mesmerized me.

The pale fading shadow of a person seemed to be walking on the wall, and a different shadow would appear and disappear. Then they got bigger and stood closer to each other. The taller shadow did not have a head.

The world was asleep. The shadows were dancing on the wall. I would confuse them with ghosts. Covering my head under the blanket, I would slowly peek out, sitting up halfway and watching them. The silence was intolerable. I was scared to scream. I would bite the corner of the blanket and could not take my eyes off the wall.

The big shadow covered the small one with its body, like a big clump of clouds that suddenly covers the sky. Then it went back, and the small shadow got closer. This time the shadow had a head, and in one instant the smaller one became like a person with a big belly and grew a head. The shadows were moving, and now an arm was separated from the entangled mass. The shadows got taller and half of them disappeared over the top of the wall, and, all of a sudden, they all fell to the ground like a black curtain. Like a little hill that disappeared in a second, resembling a passing hallucination.

Whoever the shadows belonged to originally, now they are mine. The owners did not know that they had a shadow, and that I have taken their shadows from the wall, imprisoned them, and carry them with me wherever I go. Sometimes, regardless of time and place, I get drawn in to their act. This time without the fear and horror that obscures everything. In my mind, everything is clear and the silence of the night is deep and tranquil. The pull of the shadows toward each other is soft and whimsical, and has a natural freshness. Sometimes I get tired of them though and want to return the shadows to their owners, but that is not possible. I don't know their real owners anymore.

18

Amir has fallen in love. In love with a blond woman. He introduces her to me as "my sister." The woman is thin and slender, and probably from Canada. She extends her hand and smiles. I can't tell if she is Iranian or Canadian, but she is a stranger. She can't be his sister.

I want to scream. But Amir isn't looking at me. He has turned toward the woman. No one looks at his sister like that. I am almost certain.

I squeeze my eyelids so hard that my face gets tied into knots.

I tell myself it is all over between Amir and me. I feel a sadness different from any other. I hear myself weep. It sounds like Maman's weeping.

I feel his body against mine. I have not opened my eyes yet, but I am awake. It must be almost morning. Amir has come to bed. I put my arms around him and rest my head on his neck. Reconciling silently is the best way. Amir is back and he does not know from where I have got him back.

19

The second time Aunt Mahboub sent me back, I smelled like urine. The night before, I had wet my bed, and Aunt Mahboub was fed up with me. Maman told me to go to the basement and wait for her. I was happy to be back at our own house. I did not like Aunt Mahboub's house. I was terrified of Uncle Qadir, constantly winking at me. In my nightmares, a big locust would come toward me, with a stick in his mouth. Uncle Qadir would take the hookah out of his mouth for three reasons: when he wanted to butter up Aunt Mahboub, when he wanted to wink at me, and when he wanted me to pour tea for him, so that he could hold my hand as I was serving him and blow the smoke in my face.

"You don't like your uncle?"

"I do."

He would wink. "Then why do you run away?"

"I am not running away!"

I took a step back. Maman turned the water on. Told me to get undressed. Maman was weeping and swearing. I did not know who she was swearing at, but I had learned who they were meant for by the type of swear words. Maman held the hose with cold water on my feet. I got goose bumps and shivered. The swear word that Maman used was meant for my father. Then it was her parents' turn. Aunt Mahboub had her share, too.

"Hurry up. Sit down!"

Swear words and the weight of her hand hit my bare back simultaneously. I jumped up like a frog because of the cold water, my body shivering from the cold as if I was electrified. I cried. Maman had made me black and blue.

"Stupid, hopeless girl!"

I did not say that I was scared of Uncle Qadir. I saw him searching Aunt Mahboub's purse. By moving the mouthpiece of the hookah across his neck, he let me know that if I said anything, Aunt Mahboub would cut my throat.

I had seen Aunt Mahboub beating him out of anger. She would be so angry she would hit her own head against the wall first, and then attack him. Pieces of Uncle Qadir's old white undershirt would fly in the air like the feathers of a dead bird.

Maman's swearing at people ended, and now she was cursing the heavens and the earth. She wrapped me in an old sheet and left me crumbled up in a world of fear.

20

Friday means the rumbling voice of the salt peddler, the basket vendor, and the loudspeaker of the truck that sells guaranteed sweet watermelons. Friday means loud television and Amir's long yawns. Friday means changing the old faucet and fixing the broken flush. Friday means long afternoons and picking up fights.

Like a sieve, the ceiling transfers music through its bricks and mortars and iron beams. Mr. Hashemi's daughter is dancing. You can tell by the sound of her fast steps. Amir looks at the ceiling as if he's watching a complete orchestra up there.

Shadi asks, "Maman, do you like me better or spices?"

I say, "You."

Shahin says, "They bought the tape player today. It's one of those newer models."

"Poor Hashemi, he is at the end of his rope, and they buy the latest model tape player."

Amir has discovered a new fetish, finding contradictions in people's lives.

"They rent their apartment, but go around in taxis. They are constantly fighting over money, but you can smell their expensive perfume in the stairways."

"Maman, me or ants?"

"You."

The music gets louder. Now it is not just coming through the ceiling. The walls are beating with fast foreign music.

"No matter what, we are peasants and have a village mentality. Even if they stuff every one of us inside a room, only our bodies would stay inside, our swear words would be heard outside. We hear ourselves fighting each other through the windows and the walls."

"Daddy, do you love me more, or a stone?"

"A stone. Yes, we hear each others' crying. Even our least important hopes and dreams pass through the cracks of the wall."

"Daddy, what do you love more, sugar cubes or me?"

"Sugar cubes. We know whose phone is ringing. We know who sleeps until noon, and who is awake past midnight."

"Daddy, me or a period?"

"The period, the word, the line, and the sentence."

Shahin leaves quietly.

"Do you love me more, or Ida?"

"Ida. You haven't run down batteries yet?"

"Do you love me or Ida's mom?"

"That's obvious, Ida's mom."

Ida's mom is at the door. Amir whispers, "She must have sensed that we were talking about her!"

"Can I borrow a couple of onions?"

I give her a few onions and close the door.

"There you go. All that gold on her neck, all that makeup, and she's here every day asking for a couple of onions or potatoes, or some oil."

Shadi goes to the backyard. Ebi is at the entrance of the parking lot. The kids have all gathered in the backyard and offer him coins. Ebi collects the coins and sings one of Googoosh's songs. He imitates the sound of a fire engine, the roar of a lion, and the sound of a police siren. Ebi has long hair. He is wearing an old oversized coat and cuts all the songs short. "As much as you pay," he says.

The kids clap for him and laugh. A banknote is thrown from the upper floor, and a woman says, "A Bandari dance."

Amir says, "The others pay money to enjoy it, but you get your enjoyment without paying. Haven't you had enough already?"

I move away from the window. Where should I go? Where shouldn't I go? There is no good reason to wander. If I am not standing at the window, there are only two other places I could go—either the living room or the kitchen. The backyard is at the other end of the building and the high wall there makes me feel like it's the end of the world.

I say, "I've had enough, OK?"

I have said it too late.

Amir says, "Enough of what?"

"Of everything, of this life."

Now that I have named my feeling, I realize how sad I am. Sadness has blown up like a balloon inside me. My eyes are full of tears. "Of this house, of these Fridays."

"I keep telling you that we have to leave this place."

I want to say, " . . . of you."

I don't say it. That would ruin everything. Because I don't say it, the word knocks around inside my head, "You, you, you."

"Now you agree with me."

I don't know what it is that I am agreeing with. But I feel guilty for being so fed up with him. Damn this feeling that is always with me, closer to me than a sister. Mahin and Shahla are not always with me, but this feeling never leaves me. I get close to Amir and put my head on his shoulder. It is too hard. I bring my head down to his chest. Amir caresses my hair. I think I always mislead people. Amir cannot even imagine that I am so fed up with him.

21

When Amir has had enough, he walks around the room with heavy steps like a giant. Opening and closing doors noisily. He sings in the shower, and when you least expect it, he recites poetry by Hafez.

In the mornings, he puts on his best shirt to go to work. Fixing his hair, he doesn't mind using my leftover hair color to cover his gray.

He smiles at himself in the mirror.

When he has had enough of me, my belly reminds him of a drum, and my legs of a camel. Sometimes I am transformed into a crocodile, but I always end up as a polar bear.

When he has had enough of me, he turns into a bachelor who has mistakenly become a guest in a crowded house. At times like this, the kids are no longer smart and curious, and they have not taken after their father at all. They are in the way and annoying. They eat at our brains with their irrelevant questions, and no doubt they are only my kids.

Amir treats himself and promises to do more.

"I work like a dog but dress like a beggar."

He shaves every morning and leaves the house as if he is living in a third-class motel. His cologne stays in the air for hours.

When Father had enough of Maman, he would bring home Vitamin. Vitamin was the name Father had given her. Vitamin would sing. She laughed loudly and snapped her fingers briskly. She had long black hair. Mahin said, "If she didn't have all those blemishes, she could be pretty." But Father saw the blemishes as beauty marks and recited poetry for Vitamin, and Maman took refuge in the basement because she had crystal-clear skin and no one ever read poetry to her.

Aunt Mahboub would say, "If a woman really wants poetry, she can find it even in a hellhole." She would laugh thunderously, "A woman can even make mice sing for her if she wants to."

Aunt Mahboub did not need poetry. That is why she looked at herself in the mirror a hundred times a day, not one kind of look, but a hundred; the look of a neighbor who would enter momentarily, the look of a stranger who would pass by and glance at her. Sometimes she'd look at herself as carefully as a caring and diligent doctor. She would delicately press the puffed-up bags under her eyes and would caress her neck with the same gentle touch.

When Maman had had enough, she would throw the furniture in the yard and clean everything for days while weeping. She would wipe off the doors, the walls, and the floors. She cleaned every corner of the rooms and the basement, washing everything repeatedly. Maman did not allow anyone but Shahla to go to the basement while cleaning. She said, "It is filthy everywhere. I have to disinfect the morgue."

She got rid of Uncle Qadir by using housecleaning as an excuse, and did not let him in the basement anymore. This is how Maman slowly cleared our house of the shadows. She got rid of all the ghosts, all the friends and guests, Vitamin and all the other strangers. Everything was clean and quiet after Maman was done, and Father was in the basement lying on the bed all alone, like a corpse waiting to be washed.

When Shahla has enough, she goes on a diet. She eats only almonds, pistachios, and filberts.

Maman says, "Isn't it a pity to make so much money and eat only some nuts?"

When Mahin has enough, she marries a man she doesn't even know and moves to the other end of the world.

I must be the most miserable for when I have had enough, I put my head on the stomach of the person with whom I am most fed up and listen to his stomach growl while feeling ashamed of my unhappiness.

22

Only death can turn life back to its original state. If suddenly I have a heart attack and collapse in the middle of the kitchen, Amir will notice me at last. I don't want to have an accident and end up with a deformed face. I don't want to get cancer and become weak and turn yellow. Heart attacks are better than other kinds of death. I am spread out on the floor, probably holding the spoon that I was using to stir the milk. I stare at the ceiling, but I am not dead. Amir does not know that yet.

We did not know Father had died, either. We thought he was alive, but he had died in the basement, all alone. Father loved women, pistachios, and music, but he didn't want them any longer.

"My son, bring me a piece of that red juicy thing."

Maman would sigh, and Father would say again, "Son, are you getting that red juicy thing? I am thirsty, very thirsty."

He would not remember the word for watermelon, even if his life depended on it. Mahin wanted to leave.

Shahla said, "In this cold, and at this time of the night?"

Mahin did not pay any attention to her, always trying to do the impossible. Maman blocked the basement door with her body. "He gets everything messy."

He would make a mess even without eating watermelon.

"He has left a trail. Clean him up." He had lost control before making it to the bathroom.

He would drag his feet on the floor because he could not climb the stairs.

Maman became exasperated by Father's sickness. Father should have realized by now that he could not get any sympathy by playing dead. He should die for real.

Amir should look at me now with the same concern that he had years ago, with the same love in his eyes. He should see the small wrinkles around the eyes of the woman that he will soon lose forever, and show some sympathy. He should see my eyebrows that for months everybody except him has noticed have not been plucked or shaped well. Surely he would hold my hands, and even if it wasn't a good time to compliment me, deep down he would remember that these are the same hands that got him excited once.

"Hey, where are you? The milk is boiling over."

With despair, I come back to life. I stir the milk while feeling a world of self-pity. Holding the spoon, I turn toward him and look at him with disappointment. He is bending over and examining his little toe that is dry as a bone. I wonder why a man that calls you "hey" shouldn't die. Death would certainly make him dearer, the same way that it had with Father. Mahin described him to her husband-to-be as if she was talking about Jean Valjean in *Les Misérables*, a symbol of honor and honesty. Maman also gave alms to the poor in his name.

I would cry for Amir. I would hit my chest and tear my scarf into pieces. "Amir, come back. I will die for you Amir, come back."

The women would hold my shoulders and give me sweet drinks, but I would scream, "Amir, come back. What am I going to do with these kids, Amir?"

The women that would hold my hands wouldn't know that I wanted Amir back as he was ten years ago. The same Amir that when you looked in his eyes, you would say, "Oh my God, what a beautiful color."

Amir says, "Why are you looking at me like that? Are you going crazy?"

23

 I am looking out the window. I tell Amir, "Hurry up."

Amir reluctantly comes to the window, and we both look out at the man who practices tambour in the afternoons, and now he is playing with the lock on the door.

Amir says, "I didn't think he would be so thin. He looks grumpy, too."

I say, "I don't think he's grumpy. He is just sensitive." And I want to say that he has strong hands, but I stop myself just in time. Noticing two positives at the same time is an exaggeration, and any kind of exaggeration on my part upsets Amir. I go to the kitchen.

According to Amir, people watching is a bad habit. It does not match his personality. But I love it. That's why I find the window and the peephole very useful. But now it is Amir who is not moving away from the window and is holding the curtain back.

Quickly I go to my own corner, the other side of the curtain. It is the cradle robber who is shading her face with her hand and looking at the end of the alley.

There goes a well-dressed, beautiful woman, and it is not hard to guess what is going on in Amir's head. But he always makes me doubt my talent in reading his mind. While still standing at the window, he says, "Poor thing."

"Poor who? The cradle robber or the baby?" His answer is important for me.

Amir says, "Poor me who is looking at the world through this small opening."

24

Amir wakes up and is asking for the tape that he brought back from Baku.

I say, "I'll find it later."

"No, right now."

"First sit down and have your breakfast."

Amir does not want any breakfast. He wants his tape.

I ask, "Did you have a dream?"

He does not answer, and like someone who is in a hurry, quickly goes through the drawers. I find the tape. "Here you are."

I think he should at least give me a thankful look, but it is as if I don't even exist. He puts the tape in the tape player and turns it on. The Kamancheh is playing. I sit by him. I can't ask him what he is remembering. It is impossible to figure out where Amir is right now. Is he alone or with someone else? In a concert hall or on some street? But wherever he is, I am not there. I want to bang the dishes together and make noise. I want the power to go off so that the tape player stops. A secret has crept into our house like a small animal that I don't recognize. I cannot even pet it.

I say, "It is late. Don't you want to go to work?"

He does not hear me. The echo of an ululating voice has filled the house. It's not like the birds singing. The music has brought down even the sky.

I say it louder, "You are late."

He moves away from the tape player, like a kid who is still hungry and is forced to leave the table. He wears his shoes, and looks at me as if it's my fault that I don't look like a woman he could passionately love at this moment.

25

 I write:

Dear Mahin,

Yesterday morning Shadi got your letter from the mailman and brought it home screaming happily. But she got into a fight with Shahin over opening it. I told them whoever opens the letter the other one gets to keep the stamps. Shahin immediately backed down. Shadi opened the letter. Amir said, "Let me read it."

I didn't like him reading your letter, especially out loud and full of errors. It's not a newspaper. It's a letter written only for one person. However, I didn't say anything. But the letter lost its excitement.

Dearest Mahin, I must say your letters always create a small crisis in our home. After finishing your letter, Amir says, "What a dreadful life we have." This remark belongs to evenings, when he comes home after an entire day of overtime work and collapses in front of the air conditioner, moaning. Not to the morning when it's time to go to work, and there is still opportunity to change the world.

Girl, in your letter you talk about a U.S. where everybody is living happily. Everybody thinks, talks, and lives as they wish. You talk about old women who feel young and strong, and you write about the young women who have the most beautiful smiles in the world. Shahla says, "Mahin has gone to Hollywood, not to the U.S." My problem is that I can't even imagine such a world, let alone believe in it; a world without contradictions, without suffering and regrets. But Amir believes in it, because the West, especially Canada, is his life's sole obsession. As a person who doesn't believe in anything, even if he sees it with his own eyes, now he buys any right or wrong idea about the West.

Perhaps love is inside us. I think that with love as a visa you can go anywhere and live there. But I don't really have such a permit in my pocket. I am afraid of moving over there and getting lost with my pocket empty. Then I have to beg for help. I am afraid of coming to your heaven and still seeing the traces of the hell that are stuck to me. You're right. I don't have the guts to travel. I should tell you that Amir says the same thing. When he got to this part of the letter, he applauded you.

Before I forget, I should say that Shahla wants you to write to find out if acupuncture gets rid of wrinkles around the eyes. Amir says, "Like most women, Shahla solves her problems by starting at the end." According to Amir, "Getting married is Shahla's first problem and her wrinkles are her last."

Sharing a house didn't take Maman and Shahla back to the days when they were like twin sisters and went to the basement together, whispering for hours, not fearing Father's yelling while planning to drive strangers out of the house. Shahla has been angry at the world for some time. Maman says, "It's too soon. Shahla is young and healthy and has a long way to menopause."

I say Shahla is lazy.

Maman sighs, and says, "The smart one was Mahin who went away and left everything behind."

But Maman's brightest daughter, I don't really feel jealous when you write about the most beautiful smiles of the world. Instead I need to get something off my chest. You don't remember those days. You have always lived as if life begins right now. Shahla too, God help us, nobody has yet heard her recalling a memory. A woman with no memory, she is always ready to throw around those pretty pop psychology phrases. "You have to live in the moment."

Not that her moment is very pleasant! Shahla is always complaining about her coworkers and the way Maman goes to the bathroom. But I can remember very well that one side of my face was always swollen. I often had an infected tooth that made my mouth smell horrible. When they finally took me to the dentist, the tooth had to be removed. I have so many memories of toothaches and the metal smell of the dentist's drill that I sometimes feel like I had twice as many teeth as normal people. Of course, I don't even have half of them now. To hell with not chewing well or getting stomach gas, what about my laughter? I think they ruined my smile, and not my teeth. That's why I am not upset when I cry, but I am sad when I laugh. It's impossible for the person sitting in front of you to pay less attention to your teeth than to what you're saying.

Father would see me and say, "Give me my dentures."

There was nothing more difficult than taking his dentures out of the glass and then hearing him adjusting them.

He said, "Dentures are good."

I'd look at him doubtfully. I didn't know whether he meant his dentures or something else. I couldn't even tell whether he was laughing or his dentures were out of place. His wet dentures were shiny. My tooth was aching as usual, and thinking about the near future of my teeth wasn't that comforting either. I really wanted to complain to somebody but Maman was washing clothes and weeping, and Father couldn't understand a word. There is no joy in persecuting the weak. It kills the desire to seek justice forever.

It was right then that Father said something he shouldn't have.

"Any pistachios?"

Maman hissed like a snake and got up from her washtub.

"Even if this man's heart stopped, his appetite wouldn't."

I looked at Father. Was he laughing or showing his dentures? I couldn't tell any more.

Amir was reading the letter with excitement and emotion and I was laughing. I am sure that over there foreign women cannot laugh this way. Because it's not chic at all, and it's the kind of laughter that shows discolored crowns instead of white shiny teeth.

Amir hasn't stopped reading yet. He only raised his voice like somebody who has a visitor while praying. Shahin and Shadi were staring at his mouth with their mouths hanging open.

Amir said hastily, "Hurry up. Write. I need new information. Tell Mahin to write to us."

I said, "You write."

He said, "You write better."

I frowned.

He tapped me on the shoulder, "Good job. Write. It's for our future."

26

What is the future like? The future must look like the old woman that Amir showed me in the park, like a yellow crumbled envelope. I cannot visualize the future. I don't know what it is made of. Until now, I could only imagine the future. But now that I am close enough to it, the future is losing its mystery day by day, and I want to stop it right there.

I want to stop and look at myself and my life. From far away like a lover, and close by like a stranger. I don't want to move to Canada. I don't want to spend the rest of my days adjusting to life over there because by the time I find my way around, life will be all over.

Father had put away some money for my dowry before he passed away. Shahla had announced her hatred of all relationships with the male species. Mahin had a fiancé and could not wait any longer. It was my turn to get married. As it happened, Amir asked for my hand, and very soon I joined the crowd of married women.

As soon as you get married, the first thing that happens is that a big clock is hung in your bedroom; everybody's counting the seconds to hear the big news. Then someone cooks stew with prunes for you, and another brings you sour fruit roll-ups. In the bus someone gets up and offers you their seat, and in the streets everybody unconsciously stares at your stomach that by now is big and round, meaning that it is a boy.

Then your days pass wondering about the benefits of a C-section versus natural birth. Time passes and the others begin to see in your face the changes that you already feel within. You prepare clothes for the baby in your free time, and argue with your husband about names. Then one day the pain arrives like someone you were expecting but whose arrival you couldn't believe. Fear takes over. Fear of more and more pain. You go to the hospital, and the next day they put a small and unfamiliar being in your arms that reminds you of a wet sparrow, and they ask you to breastfeed him. From that moment on, you become a mother.

On the hospital bed, you decide that one child is enough. But decisions and actions are as different as a man and a woman who are standing next to each other as strangers and pretending as if they are related. A few years pass. The thought of the death of an only child is like a lost balloon in the air, and a mother whose days are boring is the first to notice it. Then she listens to the voice of a woman who is as old as the world and whispers in her ears, "What if your only child dies?" Besides, this poor kid will always be alone, and bringing a little playmate doesn't hurt anybody, and after the parents die they would be great support for each other. Moreover, now that your work is changing diapers, and you actually have shown great aptitude in that, why not use this God-given talent to raise other kids, and a thousand other reasons. Then you get pregnant with your second child and become a complete mother.

Before you know it, wherever you go they ask about your kids, and you have to drag them with you everywhere. Your life is connected to two other human beings in every possible way. There are days that don't simply end with feeding the baby and changing diapers, the kind of days that no one has written about in any books.

Mahin takes English lessons and writes letters to the fiancé that she has never met. Shahla is busy paying the mortgage for the two-bedroom apartment that she has bought in a nice neighborhood. Now that Mahin is leaving, she can live there with Maman.

Amir is packing his backpack to seek refuge in the mountains. From this life that is filled with whining kids. He says this life bores him to death. I frown at him. The baby is feeding.

He says he is not leaving forever. He is only going to Mt. Alam for five days, and he will be back soon. Besides, it is for our sake that he is going away for such a short trip. Otherwise, he would be at the foot of Mt. Everest right now. He is a migrant bird, and for now he is trapped in a cage, but he is yearning to fly.

He says, "You are a polar bear. You like this life. It was you who gave birth to these kids, not someone else."

It is snowing. I have to give Shadi lots to drink because she has diarrhea and is running a fever. Shahin is constantly coughing. Someone has to raise the kids. This time the migrant bird has flown to Mt. Damavand. Maman is staying with me.

"Don't be so cold. Socialize with your neighbors. It is so boring here. Your last house was better."

I have to raise the kids.

"You don't have to look like you're mourning for the kids. If people didn't know better, they would think that, God forbid, the kids are sick."

I have to raise the kids.

I have to get Shadi immunized. She screams constantly. Shahin says, "Maman, we should take Shadi to the market, sell her, and be done with her."

Shadi sucks on her finger.

"Put pepper on her finger and close this door. No one is going to hear if a thief breaks in."

Shahin sits up in his bed in the middle of the night and cries out loud.

"What if my blood pressure goes up? There are no cars. No taxis."

I have to raise the kids.

Shahin makes Shadi cry, and I spank him.

Maman says, "So what that you hit him. Kids grow up by being spanked. This is not a reason for you to cry."

It *is* a reason to cry. Kids don't grow up by getting spanked. Kids don't grow up by being humiliated. They get taller, but they don't grow up.

I say this to myself.

Shahin says, "Maman, you like Shadi better than me."

It is snowing. The polar bear is sleeping under the blanket. The polar bear is telling stories for the kids. She cooks lentils for them, and in the afternoons she takes them out to play.

The polar bear is bored, bored of constantly having to take care of the kids, of the peeling walls, the broken water heater, the cockroaches that do not die with any kind of bug killer. She is tired of the long days turning to night, and of long nights that are filled with tears. The polar bear yells at the kids for no reason.

Shahla says, "You are no mother!"

I scream, "No, I am not, I am not a mother. I am a cow, a bear."

Maman says, "Why are you so cranky? It is not our fault that your husband is gone."

Shahla says, "With your temper, I don't blame him for going away."

"Yes, I cannot hold on to my husband."

I shout again. Maman gets up to leave. The kids hang on to her sleeve.

"Stay!"

Maman is upset. "No, we should be going. If we stay here any longer your Mom is going to dismiss us!"

Shahin does not know what it means to dismiss someone. But he knows that it is my fault. I have so many faults by now. They have been stacking up, one on top of the other, becoming like a heavy wet blanket that I want to pull over me and stay covered. I am not a mother, not a daughter, and not a wife. I am nothing. I cannot perform any of the roles that have been assigned to me. I was no good as a child, either. My life did not matter. Maman was hoping for a boy and I turned out to be a girl. I was a gofer for Father. He would want me only for cleaning the dandruff on his jacket, fanning and bringing coal for his hookah, clipping his toe-nails, and taking off his socks. Children for him were like the images on the hookah. He always preferred decorated hookahs over plain ones.

Mahin opens the window. It is warm and sunny.

"I'll stay with the little ones. You get out and have some fun. You need a change. Don't worry. Go get an ice cream. Do something to get out of this mood. Don't be so upset. Take a look at yourself in the mirror."

I don't like to look at myself in the mirror.

27

A woman who cheats on her husband can look like anybody except Manijeh. A woman who cheats cannot pay attention to everybody, the way Manijeh does. A woman who cheats cannot enjoy the scent of her daughter's hair and kiss her the way Manijeh does.

She says, "Why don't you take care of yourself? Why don't you ever leave this house? Why don't you come and visit us? Go shopping or to the park?"

I laugh and set the plate of cookies on the table. "You should be asking yourself these questions."

She pretends not to hear me. "You are going to get really bored and depressed."

I say, "I know, but the dead do not come back to life by going to the park or by wearing more makeup." Then I blurt out, "But maybe by falling in love."

I blush a little.

She looks at me doubtfully. I am not sure whether she doubts herself or me.

She says, "Who can find love?"

"You talk like Amir. Amir believes that love saves people, but here nobody can save anybody. Overly busy and unfortunate people start a relationship and call it love. But this is more lust than love."

It is now Manijeh's turn to blush.

"It is not just lust."

What is it then I want to know?

I am thinking about treating her with coffee instead of the usual tea, but I want her to come clean first.

To make her talk, I say, "Maybe it is companionship, short-term relationships like going for short trips."

I remember my own imaginary trips. "I can't really call them trips; they are more like going a little further than the park."

She sighs, "I don't know."

Now it is my turn to doubt. Maybe Manijeh doesn't even have what I think she is hiding like a jewel. She only has a sick husband with a dark, suspicious heart.

In that case, I should make her some coffee. That is what I do. Singing, I walk barefoot in the kitchen from one side to the other. Manijeh has brought the plate close to her face and is staring at the pattern. The kids are playing a noisy game.

She says, "What an interesting plate!"

I don't understand what she means. I look at the plate in her hand. She laughs.

"He will leave you. You know he will. You should leave first before you are left alone and turn into a loser."

She fans herself with the plate.

I feel I shouldn't say anything. Her trust is not complete. She may get scared and pull in like a turtle. I nod my head, pretending that I understand her, but in reality, I don't.

So, a few minutes later I say, "It won't happen by changing where you live. You will have the same problems in the next place."

"How do you know?"

She is right. How do I know? How many times have I changed houses? How would I know what I'll be like in another life?

28

Shadi is doing her homework. "Maman, what do you want to be when you grow up?"

I say, "Don't chew on the pencil."

She takes the pencil out of her mouth. "OK. Tell me."

"I am already a grown-up."

Now she has put the pencil in between her toes.

"I have already become what I wanted to be."

Shadi takes the pencil out of her toes.

"Maman . . ." She pushes her bangs away. "Be serious."

I think, "Well, . . . I want, I want . . ."

All of a sudden I say, "I want to be a dancer."

Amir lifts his head up from the newspaper and looks at me. I repeat what I said, and ask Shahin to put some music on so I can start practicing immediately. I get up and dance. First I imitate Mahin. The kids laugh. They clap and Shadi jumps up and down like a monkey. They ask for another dance. "Imitate Aunt Ashraf!" I push the table aside to make more room. The kids have stopped doing their homework. The house is filled with joy.

Amir says, "You should have said 'a clown.'"

Now, I quit imitating and start dancing like I used to. Imagining I am dancing in a special and unfamiliar place makes me excited. For a few seconds I forget where I am. I am twirling so fast that no one can even catch up with me.

All of a sudden I stop. "Have I become what I wanted?"

I am frozen like a windup doll that all of a sudden goes completely unwound, with my arms still stretched open.

Shahin yells, "Maman should dance."

The kids are getting rowdy. They have turned up the music. I bend over shaking my hair like when I get out of the shower. Starting again, I dance even faster than before.

29

"Maman! Amir is leaving."

"His bird has flown away. He can't stay here any longer. He has to follow his bird. Let him go."

Maman says that everybody has a bird. When the bird flies away and lands somewhere, it calls out for its owner to follow.

Amir's bird has landed in Baku. It has flown ahead and is waiting for him. Baku is not way out there. It is close by. It is only a few hours drive.

"I will send letters. I will call. I will come and visit you once a month."

"Don't go, Amir. I can't. The kids are too young."

"Think of their future. Life is not only about today. Tomorrow we won't be able to meet even their simplest needs. You cannot find these kinds of opportunities every day. Leaving is the only option."

"Stay so you can come home at night."

Amir hugs me without saying a word. He has made up his mind. I know that his bird has gone ahead of him and is waiting at the Metro station in Baku. He wants to fly away too. And see new places. Experience a different life.

"You should live your own life, too. Don't be so dependent on me. I will send you money. Take care of the kids."

He starts packing his bag while whistling a song that is not for me anymore. Amir can manage without me, but why can't I do the same? I can't. Already I am dreading the long afternoons without him.

Amir says, "The future is dark, very dark. The only way out is my work, especially now that I am still young and have energy. There is no other way. I have to go."

Amir's bird has flown to Baku ahead of him and is awaiting its owner.

30

Shahla is on a diet. I serve her salad without dressing, with lots of dill.

She's talking about the architecture of our house. "The bathroom is out of sight and near the shower. That's good."

I ask about her coworkers. But Shahla insists on talking about the bathroom. Talking about the flush and how big the toilet is.

You can't walk ahead of Shahla. You have to wait and move at her pace.

"There is enough room to even add a European toilet."

Shahla always has a ritual. She has her own system and has to do everything her way in order to get to where she wants. I am trying to figure out her new routine. She always follows her rules. Maman says, "Even as a little girl, she had her very own plate, and when she played house there were so many regulations that the other kids got tired, and she was forced to offer tea to herself. At bedtime she rearranged her sheets and blankets many times."

To this date, the fluffiness of her pillow is a matter of life and death. She would easily cancel a trip if she did not have her own special sheets.

"At home I can read and take care of my paperwork. I can listen to the news, but only if Maman is not leaving the bathroom with a few drops of water dripping down her leg. She ought to dry herself off after using the toilet."

I must be staring at her.

She says, "I am talking about legs. Wet legs drive me nuts. Do you understand what those little drops of water do to me? You don't know how I feel when I get that upset."

I know when she is nervous, she plays with her pimples to the point that they go away. She sits in front of the mirror and tweezes her eyebrows until the light skin underneath shows. She files her fingernails so sharp that they look like the tip of a fountain pen with no ink.

She inspects every corner of the house and keeps talking about the toilet and the sink. I am hopeful, because I have found something that I can talk to Shahla about, and perhaps I can share something about Amir, too, the fact that I have not yet been able to accept his departure. Canada is not like Baku in that he can come back any time he wants to. Canada is on the other end of the world, and the world is only becoming smaller for the rich. For us it remains big, very big. I am getting into details when Shahla moves her double chin and walks toward the bathroom. That's not only a piece of flesh hanging from her chin. A delicate movement of her double chin tells you that she is not interested in sentimental stories, and she is determined to only talk about toilets and sinks.

Shahla is not interested in just anything in the world. Other people's emotions keep her attention as long as they fit into her sewing pattern. Shahla is all about patterns, customs, plans, and logic.

To be her sister, you have to accept her ways. Once she was a devout believer, then a strong supporter of free elections, and later she turned into a vegetarian. After Father's death, she put away all these beliefs. She no longer followed any ideas. For a long time she became indifferent. But being indifferent was hard work for her. Having any kind of commitment was unbearable for her if you wanted to get close to her.

Shahla says, "I can't watch TV. All my attention is on those wet legs. I can't put on makeup, and the room does not smell good even after using all that soap and perfume. Sometimes I want to throw everything away."

That's what she did with the basement. One day, she brought in a secondhand buyer and gave away all the furniture. Against Maman's protests, she gave the trunks to the neighborhood thrift shop and replaced them with metal shelves. She mounted them on top of Father's bed, which had been moved to the basement. She arranged Father's medications on the shelves. The basement looked like a makeshift hospital in a war zone. Then she bought an air freshener and sprayed it on the door every day, as if she were writing dangerous graffiti.

"Our bathroom is right by the kitchen in full view of everybody."

As if I have not seen her house.

"Where the TV is and it's impossible not to see who is leaving the bathroom."

She shuddered as if she were disgusted with something. Her body shivered for a moment.

"Old age is a bad thing. I want to live only as long as I have control over my body and can come out of the bathroom dry and decent."

Shahla opens the bathroom door and looks inside with interest. "Have you noticed in the bathroom where the hose for cleaning yourself is, and how accessible it is? Even a child can easily wash himself, let alone a grown-up."

I nod and realize that I have never given a thought to the hose in the bathroom in all my life.

Shahla says that the door to our bathroom is not like theirs. That although their door is very fancy, it is narrow and makes it difficult to get in and out. She turns her face and her double chin toward me and says, "I can't take it anymore. Maman knows it too. I've had it."

31

Maman says, "I can't take it anymore."

She could not put up with Father.

Father did not want to be confined in the basement anymore. He wanted to get out. "I want to go and buy one of those tall black things."

Mahin says, "I will buy you a Coke."

"No, I have to go there myself."

"Where is there?"

He could not remember how to say where he wanted to go. He said, "Help me remember." The name of the place was on the tip of his tongue, like hot food. It was as if his tongue was burning. He was stuttering.

He put his foot in one shoe and threw his jacket on his shoulder. "I have to go there."

"Where the hell is there?"

He grabbed Mahin's hand. "Take me there!"

"Where the hell do you want her to take you?"

Maman was beyond herself.

"There is water there. It is not dark."

I said, "Park?"

He repeated "Park! Park!"

He asked me to say it again. "No, no that is not it."

Maman was pounding on his pillow. "Lie down."

Father looked at Maman with fear, and held Mahin's hand tightly. "I have to go."

Maman screamed. "Go, go and leave us alone. Then go! Hurry up and get the hell out of here."

Father looked at us one by one, though with no recognition. His mouth was half-open, and his dentures were pushing out. His eyes narrowed. We were all looking at him. He was crying.

32

"You're like glue, superglue."

I wait, and when Amir comes I cling to him.

"Stay. Don't leave again. I can't take it any longer."

Amir is happy and full of energy. He kisses my face again and again.

"One day I'll take you all there."

"Take us now," I beg.

Amir gets edgy.

"Don't cling to me like this. Stay here close to you for what . . . to die of hunger? Can't you see where we're heading? Have you gone blind? We have frightening days ahead of us, horrible and dark days."

I get out of the house. If I stay, I'll hate myself, him, the house, and even the children. I leave milk and food for the kids and let Amir know. I have to get going. It's getting dark. My clingy kids follow me with their eyes. Amir has to divert their attention so I can get out of the house. But Shadi notices and screams.

It has been snowing steadily since last night. It's dark. Passing a few alleys, I get to the main street. It is lit in the main street and the bright lights of the market can be seen from far away. I cover my mouth with the corner of my shawl and walk toward the noise and the light. As I walk I feel less worried. What a blessing not to worry about the kids, to be able to go for a walk, even in such cold weather, in a snow that will soon turn into slush. It's been a long time since I have stepped out of the house alone. Isn't it better to go back right now? No, I won't.

I cling. Maman doesn't. That's what Father used to tell her, "pretty, but cold."

Maman never got attached to anything. Not to Father, not to the house, not to her children. When we sat next to her, she became restless. "Don't lean on me. Get away."

She liked to walk in the streets by herself. In the public bathhouse, she sat us on the bench and told the attendant to watch out for us. She would go in and then called us in one by one. When Father wasn't home, she made her bed some distance from us, and when he was there, she made her bed away from Father's. In the bus, she didn't like her body rubbing against other women's bodies.

Now I am in the market. It's not as busy as usual. A few women with lots of makeup are standing in front of a store window. Talking and laughing. It's warm in the market and the stores are brightly lit. I use the escalator going up and come down using the back steps. I walk with the crowd, and I am forced to move slowly. All my fears are left outside the market.

Everybody is alive. They walk, talk, and laugh. Nobody pays any attention to me. I enter a store and ask the price of a yellow hat for a child. My face feels warm. Everybody is alive. Only I have died because I have no place to go. I have to stay in that house all alone with children who know nothing. They just want milk and food. They want clean clothes and toys.

In my mind I send Amir away from the house. He has to leave for the sake of the future. I put myself in the center of the house. But I must stay. I can't go with two little kids to a foreign place and wander around. So we must stay put.

But nights arrive late and the days know no rules or laws for ending. Amir is chasing the future. There are no guarantees. He may bring the future with him, or he may not. The past is a wreck and that doesn't help. The house is poor and smells like medicine and baby milk. The carpet is covered with toys. I have to separate the small ones. Shadi may put them in her mouth.

I leave the market. It's late. It's still snowing lightly. A man is selling cooked beets. The steam is rising. There are many trucks around the market. Trucks full of oranges, tangerines, and sweet lemons. I turn into the alley. The noises are distant now, and it's dark and quiet in the alley. There is only the whiteness of the snow and the light from a few streetlamps. I am walking carefully, but I slip and fall. Nobody is in the alley. I have to get up. My back hurts. I clench the snow and tears fill my eyes. Even all that glow and color couldn't relieve the pain that I am now throwing up like undigested food. Now I understand why I have left the house at this time of the night. I have left the house to be alone and hear myself make a promise, a promise never ever to cling again, never again be dependent. I get up and start walking toward the house.

33

It's two days since Amir's bag is empty. He has no stories or news. He eats his dinner and stares at the television screen. When I talk, he doesn't listen. He doesn't even answer when I ask him a question. The third day, he hits Shadi for a petty excuse and yells at me for spending money when everything is so expensive. It's my turn to get up and say, "Which money? What expense?" I say that for months I've had to make do with these old clothes and haven't said a word.

"Tell me what makeup I have bought? What purse or shoes have I purchased? What have I bought for the children?"

It's my turn to say something, but I let Amir talk, complain, and yell. Maybe I can find out what's wrong by reading between the lines. But he doesn't talk. How can I peek into his world?

I point to the kids to be quiet. I must calm everything down. I must do something so that Amir will talk. I make up the beds and tell the kids to go to bed quietly. I turn down the TV and sit by Amir. He is laying on his stomach. I rub his shoulders. Often in the evenings, Amir promises money, fun, and a visit to the park to get the kids to massage him. His eyes are closed. It's no use. He's asleep.

I think how stupid of me to think that I know everything about Amir, that I know him like the palm of my hand, that there is nothing in his life that I don't know about. The face of this tired and sullen man becomes even more unfamiliar.

Just like when Father returned home after a day of wandering and did not look anything like the man who had left the house. There was no way to figure out what had happened to him that day, how his day had gone, and what kind of a person he'd been.

Amir is a stranger and he is absent. Whoever he was today, he couldn't have been happy. Because if he was, it would have rubbed off on us too. Whenever Father came home, he stood by the door miserable and drained, just like a merchant who has just found out that he's bankrupt.

I lay down close to Amir. Right now, I am not his wife, his mother, or his sister. We have no connection. The cold, white glare of the TV, like a spotlight from the enemy line, identifies us. We have collapsed on the carpet like two strangers. I cling to Amir and hold on tight to his shoulders. He turns over and hugs me in his sleep. We are not husband and wife. Neither is he a man, nor am I a woman. We are simply two people seeking comfort in each other's arms.

34

Shahla, Mahin, and Maman want to go home. They came over this afternoon and now its night, the beginning of the night, a little after sunset. Shahin is hanging on to Mahin's arm. "Take me too."

Shadi is sucking on her finger. Maman has lifted up her heavy body and is straightening her dress. "I'll stay if you're scared."

"No, no, I am not scared."

Mahin tells Shahin, "Go get changed and let's go."

Shahla is at the door, shining her shoes. She is in a rush. Has work to do.

She says, "We can't. He'll want his mother. We can't bring him back in the middle of the night."

Mahin says, "Shahin is not a kid. He is a man."

I say, "Mahin dear, it's okay. It's a hassle to take him and bring him back."

Shahin is crying.

"If we take you, your mother will be all alone."

That's what Maman says.

Shahin is crying. Maman takes out some money from her purse. Shahin throws down the money.

Maman says, "Okay, go get changed and come back."

Shahin has taken out his clothes from the drawer. "Maman, where are my socks?"

He has put on one sock halfway and is holding the other one in his hand. He is not looking at me. He is embarrassed about leaving me alone. He comes to the living room. I notice that the ceiling is too high and the light very dim. The shadow of the chandelier is cast on the walls. The faucet in the kitchen is dripping. Shadi is holding on tight to my hand.

I say, "Shahin, Sweetheart, I myself will take you out tomorrow."

Shahin searches the rooms, the bathroom, too. He looks down from the stairway. There is nobody. He looks out the window. He is not tall enough to see the end of the street. He returns to the room, kicking the closed door and screams, "Jerks!"

35

 I feel the tremors of this life. I can smell the whiff of separation. Life will change. We could do anything, but still not be able to stay together as we are. I make a soup. Soup reminds Amir of his mother. A mother who could be summed up in two words: devoted and hardworking. But my mother couldn't be defined even by a thousand words. I make spaghetti and cutlets for Shahin and Shadi. Everybody should leave a table full and satisfied. Everybody should enjoy their food. Doesn't everybody try to have what we have, enough food and a life together?

There is a celebration at our house, and I am the only one who knows about it. It is a feast to preserve the moment, a moment that will probably not be there tomorrow. I feel the turbulence under my feet. I smell separation.

Patiently I listen to Shahin's silly jokes. Shadi doesn't want to be left behind either. "A boy was walking on his hands. Somebody asked him, 'Why are you walking on your hands?' The boy said, 'Because my father has said I am not allowed to put a foot in the street.'"

Shahin says, "Ha, ha, very funny!"

But I laugh wholeheartedly. This little man and woman who are close to beating each other up bring me so much joy, and Amir doesn't know why he feels like telling a joke that's not really funny, and doesn't know why he's teasing the kids. He doesn't know why he joins Shahin to make fun of Shadi. Now I have to play my usual role and come to Shadi's rescue and tell them, "Don't be so mean." Amir and Shahin keep at it and turn into real monsters and laugh harder. Amir, Shadi, and Shahin don't realize they are participating in a feast that I have arranged. This is a celebration of life and sitting together at the table; I laugh heartily, feeling the passage of every second.

36

In his letters Amir writes about Azerbaijani people, about Baku, the boulevards, and the underground metro. He writes about museums, statues, and the libraries. In response I write about the weather, the newspaper reports, and the new highways that the government is building, about the supermarket that has opened recently, the gas pipelines, and the farmer's market.

Every other day, I shop at the market with the kids. Going there is a journey in itself. Going to the bazaar is a journey too. Going to Shahla's house at the other end of the town is a journey. I fill my bag with snacks, lemonade, fruit, and chocolate. The kids are allowed to ask one hundred questions till we get to where we want. They can talk as much as they want. They can run after each other and even collect pebbles. They can ask for grilled corn or ice cream.

Shadi draws a picture for Amir. Shahin writes a few lines, and after greetings, I tell him about the landlord's message. "I won't extend the deadline. We need the house ourselves. You must leave by the end of the month."

In fifteen days, this place will no longer look like a house. It'll be storage filled with boxes placed on top of each other, with packed furniture. Life will stop. I have to look for a new apartment. We have to move.

Amir can't quit his work to come back home. The kids have to keep walking.

"I'm tired, Mom."

Walking is good. It's always been rewarding. It's certainly useful when you're poor and the taxis are expensive, or when you're rich and you lose weight by walking. If you want to think, you can walk. If you want to empty your mind of thoughts, walking helps. To appreciate life, you should walk in busy streets. To forget people's unkindness and malice, you should walk, when you're young and when you're old. When you're a kid, every stop means something delicious, and to get to the next stop you should keep walking.

The kids are walking ahead of me. When they get tired, they fall behind. When all three of us feel good, we walk hand in hand.

Father always walked ahead of everybody. Maman and the kids fell behind. Shahla would always pull me, and Mahin wanted to walk farther back to jump and play. The back of Father's coat was my only target. I was afraid of getting lost if I lost track of his coat.

But Amir isn't like him. He gets bored walking by himself. He wants me by his side in order to do two things at the same time. Amir always hits many targets with one bullet. It's a waste to use one bullet for each target. When he eats, he watches TV too. When visiting relatives, he wants to run a couple of errands on his way. What's he doing now?

My masochism has found an excuse and is singing happily. Amir is walking shoulder to shoulder with a woman in the streets of Baku that he says are clean and wide. I wait till the sting of jealousy goes deep through my body like an electric current. I look again at the picture that I have imagined. It is so clear that it almost looks real. Baku's sun is bright and bountiful, and the trees in the streets are very tall.

I don't go any further. I freeze the scene right there to get my revenge by holding on to the most familiar shot. I conjure up a man by my side, and I start talking to him about the houses I have seen, about the agencies I have visited. I take out a bunch of colorful business cards from my pocket to show him.

"These are business cards from the rental offices."

I am not happy at all about the high prices. How expensive. And besides, we have to look for an apartment on the first floor so the kids can run around. I feel like chatting and realize how much you can talk about a trivial subject. I look around. The kids have fallen behind. There is no sign of a man.

Despairingly I tell myself if Amir is having a good time with another woman in that street next to the metro station, nothing in the world could ruin it. My brain is like a sieve with large holes; dreams and hallucination pass through it and attack my mind. I can't think straight. I am moving and staying put at the same time. Ultimately, one thought is more persistent than others: the image of a man and a woman in love.

But I have learned how to handle my imagination that is gliding around me like a butterfly, showing off its wings that change color every second. I remain still for the butterfly to get close. I wait till it gets closer and even closer. Cross-eyed, I stare at its locust-like body.

The search is successful; we are in a new apartment.

A few days have passed, and I still haven't found my favorite spot in this new place. This usually takes a day or two. Once I found my special corner right away. But a few days have passed and no corner of this place feels familiar to me yet. It's not kind. I walk from room to room, moving things around, and it still feels like it is not taking shape.

The bedroom is all set, the bed, the mirror, and the dresser. I want to lean on the pillow. I did it, but I realize that I can't think about Amir, about Baku, about the future. I can't think of anything. Sometimes, the problem is simply that the kitchen is too small, and at other times, it's that the room doesn't have any wall space to lean on. Sometimes, it's because the bathroom fan makes a horrible noise. I try it all. I check every corner of the house. Something has to be moved around.

Shahin can't read the first letter that Amir has written for him. Holding the letter, he is following me, and I have to correct his reading.

"It's not prinkapuls. It's principles."

Shahin reads one word and I read the other.

"Goal."

I tell Shahin to wait till later.

"Pride."

His words hit the back of my head like rocks.

"Hard work and persistence."

My head feels heavy. I lie down on the floor in the middle of the living room. I feel I have fallen in a merry-go-round and I am turning around. I think my dream is flawed. Like that cracked piece of china that I didn't want to throw in the garbage, but I know it's of no use any longer. The merry-go-round that I am riding on can't take me far away. I keep turning and yet remain in the same spot.

"Mom, what's wrong?"

I say, "Nothing. I'll get up after I rest a little."

But I want to say, "To hell with this house."

37

I am running a fever. Maman was supposed to stop by, but she didn't. Her feet hurt too much. Shahla called a few times and said I should go to the doctor. She says I shouldn't have let Amir leave and have fun by himself in Baku while I am left alone with two kids. I don't say anything.

By late night my body is on fire. Maman didn't come. The phone doesn't ring any more. Shahin and Shadi are sitting by my side. I tell them I can't get up, and they should go to the fridge and find something to eat.

I close my eyes. When I open them everything is clean and organized. The kids have put things away. Shahin has brought a wet cloth, putting it on my forehead. Shadi is trying hard to remove my socks. Shahin tells her to leave my socks alone and get a glass of water for me. Their tiny little hands move all over my body. They talk very quietly with each other and are careful not to wake me up. I am shivering.

I am in a swimming pool that has no water. I say, I have come here to swim. Why isn't there any water? A few fat women are all dressed and sitting around the pool, but they don't talk to me. They are cleaning vegetables and dumping them in the pool that by now looks green and slimy. The air is hot. I have come a long way to swim in the pool. I want to get my body wet but there is not even one drop of water.

Holding their heads down, the fat women are cleaning vegetables in silence. I scream, "Water." My lips are dry. I open my eyes. The kids have thrown a couple of blankets on me and are fast asleep at my feet.

38

Amir says, "You've become really fat, like a buffalo. I like the slim girls who stroll in the streets, thin and slender."

I laugh. I gently stroke my arm. It's silky and smooth. My hand should remain on my arm to feel its softness. If I remove my hand, I might think I have the skin of a rhinoceros, the thick skin of a rhinoceros that would mistake hitting for caressing.

I laugh.

If a marriage lasts, the woman becomes tough. On the surface the skin feels smooth, but it is becoming thick. This woman doesn't pass out or faint. Neither does she agonize day and night. She doesn't beat herself up, sleep hungry at nights, or want to kill all the slim girls.

I laugh.

Not a nervous laughter, but a happy one, happiness for what makes any woman rich: self-confidence.

My silence further agitates Amir, because his skin has become thin and my loud laughter passes through it and penetrates his heart.

"What are you laughing at, chubby?"

39

My belly might get bigger. Mahin's hips might grow bigger. One day we may look in the mirror, see our faces, and feel sorry for ourselves. One day Mahin may no longer be able to dance so energetically, and perhaps one day I will become less patient and surrender to fate. Destiny can do whatever it wants with me.

That's why Shahla forces me to go for walks with Mahin. Because all these horrible things may happen to us. As we occasionally walk shoulder to shoulder, I feel that anxiety is pushed away. I say, "To hell with hip and belly."

I think out loud, "It's our soul that needs air."

Mahin objects, "But not this polluted air. This is dirty. There is also too much noise. You know what I want?"

Mahin doesn't talk about what she wants; she acts it out. Now, she is extending her arms. "Clean air."

It's like a dance. Her hands almost reach the ground.

"Clean earth refreshed by rain." She pushes her arms forward. "And a bicycle."

Now she is biking. I have been left behind. Even as a child, she was always too smart to get stuck in any kind or unkind person's web. She always managed to get away.

"Lady athlete, what about me?"

"What do I want you for? I want a sweetheart."

A strong, well-built man passes by. I say quietly, "Here is your sweetheart."

Mahin says, "You're a woman with no dreams," and that's why she is sorry for me.

But I don't give up. "So, who else looks good?"

And I look at the faces of every single man in the park. But Mahin's love doesn't look like any of these men. Her love wouldn't burp or scratch himself; he wouldn't stare or curse. He would just bike by her side. I will wait till her sweetheart gets off his bicycle. The bicycles finally have to stop somewhere.

Mahin says, "Now he smiles at me and asks me, 'Are you tired, my dear?'"

"But I think he smiles and says, 'Honey, what's for dinner?' And the sound you hear isn't coming from his loving heart. I hate to disappoint you but the sound comes from a little lower, from his empty stomach."

After dinner, the sweetheart's eyes become heavy and his yawns are as big as the pictures in the dentist's office. I'll point out that yawning has one positive outcome. It reminds you that your sweetheart has a cavity, and you have to pay for it with your next paycheck.

Mahin says, "Poor you, you hear the sound of yawning and I hear soft music after dinner."

"But dishes, dishes, honey, dishes."

Mahin says, "Shut up. You're mean and jealous. God help Amir. You ruin everything."

I say, "I'm sorry. I don't want them to write in your obituary 'unfulfilled young woman.'"

She starts walking fast, "And I am sorry for you because that's all you see. That will be exactly what you get in life, and nothing more."

40

I put the kids to sleep. Leaning on the wall, I stretch my legs as if I have returned from a very long trip and not from Shahla's house. My back hurts and my mind is preoccupied. I have no choice but to return and live with my kids.

I change Shadi's diaper. Shahla is watching my hands to make sure I wash them carefully. She walks behind Shahin and picks up the junk on the carpet. I seat the kids next to me to make sure they don't get the table dirty, and don't pound on the door with the palm of their hand, or that they don't touch the phone, or make noise with the knife and plate. Shadi likes to walk on the couch, and she makes the cover fall off every time. The clean kitchen floor makes Shahin excited, and he wants to slide on it.

I want to help Maman and Shahla with cooking. They say it's better if I watch after my kids to make sure they don't do anything wrong. At lunch I make sure they don't put the yogurt spoon on the table cloth, don't spill rice, and hold their glasses carefully.

Maman says, "Put the kids to sleep so we can all take a nap."

She brings a pillow and tells them to keep quiet; otherwise the boogeyman from downstairs will come up and eat them. The kids can't sleep. They want to play. Shadi crawls under the couch. Shahin is bored and whiny.

I am back in my own house. I tell myself I'll stay right here till the kids grow up. I won't go anywhere anymore. We'll stay here within these walls, the three of us. It's as if for the first time I face the reality of my life. As if only tonight I am able to throw away such nonsense like a shared life, the warm family unit, and other rubbish, and make up my own definitions. This is my life and these two kids belong only to me. Now I have all the responsibility to continue as I see fit. The heavy pain makes me wipe away my tears. I feel I have become stronger.

41

Mahin squeezes Shadi and makes her scream. Then she gets up and plays dodge ball with the kids. Shahla laughs, "Big kid!"

Maman watches Mahin and her eyes fill with tears. These days Mahin sings. She shops and speaks English. She writes letters. Makes a list of things she wants to take with her, and now she has turned to the kids.

"What do the little ones want their aunt to send them from abroad?"

Shahin says, "A gun."

Shadi says, "I want a gun too."

Shahin quickly says, "Monkey see, monkey do. Are you a monkey?"

Mahin teases Shahla. "Come on, tell me: shampoo, soap, lotion, toothpaste, perfume, and . . ."

"There is no need. I buy them here. The Iranian ones are better."

Mahin says, "You don't like to spend money, Miss Stingy."

Maman says, "Thank God, she does have money."

Shahla laughs, "I am saving for a rainy day."

Mahin wrinkles her nose.

"What's a rainy day anyway?"

"It's a cloudy and sad day. Somebody might die on a day like that."

Maman whispers, "Dear, I have money for my own funeral."

Mahin raises her voice, "If somebody dies on such a day, it won't be a rainy day. It will be a day of mourning. Can you tell me what use you have for money on a mourning day?"

"There might be a day when only money can prevent a disaster. There must be a day that I can let go of my savings after all, because there won't be a tomorrow to worry about."

Shahin has changed his mind. "I don't want a gun. I want a sailboat."

Mahin brings her eyebrows together the way she usually does and makes her mouth look small and beautiful. "What about you, pretty girl?"

Shadi looks at Shahin. Shahin is giggling. He knows that Shadi doesn't know what a sailboat is. Shadi takes her finger out of her mouth and laughs, "A balloon."

Everybody laughs. Mahin looks at me.

I say, "I don't need anything."

"You're taking it too seriously. Say something."

Shahin is hanging from my neck, "Say something, Maman."

I look down. I think about what I want. I don't know. I want to say something. I want to laugh. I hold my head up, "Letters." I bite my lips. I know my nose has turned red. Mahin comes closer. She hugs Shahin and me together and starts sobbing.

42

A love letter has arrived from Amir. He has written that only when you are far from your everyday life do you begin to realize what you actually had.

He has written that he is only beginning to appreciate me, and that he misses home and the kids. He can't work like he used to and besides, with winter coming, work won't be profitable any longer.

He has written that he is lonely most of the time. His neighbor invites him over once in a while. They are hospitable people. Their daughter plays piano for him, and he remembers me in those moments.

Shahla says, "Amir is farsighted. He can only see things from a distance. When he gets closer . . ."

I say, "Everything gets blurred."

"No, everything is crystal clear. But Amir is blind."

Shahla is waiting for me to agree with her. I should throw my vicious memory at the wall. I have to remember everything. All those hurt feelings, all the feuds. Where did all that hatred go? But my memory works magic. Everything has vanished, and I feel guilty for wishing that Shahla would leave as soon as possible so I can read Amir's letter again and again.

43

I don't write Amir about highways and the new construction. Neither do I write about the supermarket that drove away the customers from the very beginning. I write about me and the world around me, about every corner of our new house. I write about the landlord, and Shahin and Shadi who are growing up and becoming sweet.

You can hear Shadi's voice from every corner of the house. She talks, sings, and makes up stories. You can hear her singing even when she is in the bathroom washing her hands.

Shahin says he is the man of the house, and everybody should obey him. He puts on Amir's winter hat. Wears his coat and walks around the room. Shadi laughs hard.

"I order you . . ."

He turns to me and doesn't know what orders to give. His finger is left in the air.

"I order that . . ."

Shadi joins him and gives orders too. Unclear orders are floating over my head. Shahin screams. He has found an order after all.

"I order you to laugh."

You can't disobey an order given with so much effort. I laugh. To follow his next order, I get up and we chase each other and play. At night I feel like a queen with my devoted ministers sleeping by my side.

I continue writing to Amir. I write that we are all well, and he'd better not misbehave like the kids. He should stay there till the end of the winter and finish his job.

44

Shahla's maman says, "A man shouldn't take off and leave his wife and small children all alone."

But my maman says, "The farther a pest, the less problematic life is."

Shahla's maman says, "A woman who has an income or a salary doesn't need a husband."

But my maman says, "It's better to at least have the name of a husband anyway."

Mahin writes that they raised us as the sons who were never born, and among us Shahla is the worst victim. She became neither a man nor a woman. She is male.

Shahla's maman doesn't eat breakfast.

"I have no appetite."

And to convince herself she says, "A big breakfast is not good for you."

But my maman stops her weeping after everybody leaves the house, like a radio that is suddenly turned off. Then she sets the table. Brews the tea and is careful the tea has a nice color and flavor and doesn't taste like bath water. She puts preserves, walnuts, and cheese in separate dishes and eats her breakfast as she watches the sparrows outside her window.

Shahla's maman is a thoughtless woman who has reached this age without saving a single penny. My maman has so much savings that nobody knows the exact amount, and in those evenings when she feels down and nobody is around, she brings it out. Counting her money over and over, she wraps a thick rubber band around each bundle.

Shahla's maman is an old woman who thinks about the other world, but my maman has only recently found time to think about this world.

Shahla's maman is a woman who tolerated all kinds of misery and remained faithful to her husband to the end, but my maman remained loyal to herself more than anybody else.

When Shahla talks about Maman I listen quietly. The woman Shahla talks about is only her maman.

She waves her hand in front of my eyes and snaps her fingers. "Where are you?"

I say, "With Mahin. I miss her."

And I don't tell Shahla that I had gone to Mahin to talk about the maman I knew.

45

I write:

Dear Mahin

Maman is sick. Shahla is supposed to get the results of Maman's tests tomorrow. She thinks it's better for Maman to lose some weight. Maman quietly says, "She wants to kill me with hunger."

I bring Maman home with me for a few days. The neighbors come to visit her. Amir advises, "Don't let those people come in the house."

Maman says, "The son of a government minister is not as stuck-up as your husband."

Maman is weeping and puts her hand on her chest. "It hurts here. It hurts a lot."

I remember Aunt Mahboub. She also used to put her hand on her heart saying it hurt. I remember well that her hand wouldn't go down. Instead she would move her hand toward her necklace, fixing it on her cleavage. Rubbing her throat, she would ask, "Do you know how to get rid of these tiny freckles?"

She had traits that Maman doesn't. Maman is not made of the same clay.

She says, "I am afraid to have a heart attack like Mahboub."

Maman is submerged in her thoughts.

You can't tell if she is thinking about Aunt Mahboub's death or her own.

"What's the use of being alive like Qadir?"

The neighbors would hear Uncle Qadir's sobbing through the night calling for Aunt Mahboub.

"Or like that blessed soul." Then she says, "Peace upon him."

Which one of the dead is she blessing, I ask?

"Mahboub. My poor sister. It wasn't her time yet."

Perhaps she will give a second blessing too. But no. Nobody is here to pretend for. It's only me and her. Like the night that Maman and I were awake. You were not home. Shahla was asleep.

In the moonlight I could see that she was awake and I could hear Father's voice. His voice was coming from the basement. It wasn't a cry for help, but it was the voice of someone who was begging for something and could be heard very well in the silence of the night. How long I stayed like that, I don't know. I was wishing for the moaning to stop. I covered my head with the blanket but could still hear him moan. I waited for Maman to get up, but she kept lying there listening.

It was the sound of crying. It was the sound of pleading and weeping. The sound of pain. I half rose and got closer to Maman. Her eyes were closed. But I knew she was awake. I had seen her eyes gleam. I called her. She didn't answer. I wanted to go downstairs, but I didn't dare. I thought it was a dream that would end, like a nightmare that would be forgotten. Everything would come to an end. It would end right then. But it didn't.

I shook Maman's shoulders. She turned her back to me and sobbed. I was afraid of waking up Shahla. She'd be cranky for a few days if she didn't get her sleep. I sat in my bed.

You know Mahin, to make up for that night I throw the pillow off of my face every night in my dream and go to the basement by myself. I turn the lights on and sit by Father.

I still haven't been able to forgive myself for lying down in bed hiding my head under the pillow. This is one of tens of images in which I don't like myself, and one can't get over something like that without love. I am stuck behind these images, on the side of the shadows, and I own all of them. How can a person get anywhere bearing all this weight?

Father died that same night, lonely, like a defenseless child.

I can't write any more. I fold the letter, and put it under my mattress.

46

I have found my favorite place in the house. I am sitting there and flipping through a book. I go back to the beginning of the line and read the same sentence over and again. My eyes, like magnets that have lost their power, only move on the paper without absorbing the words. I rest my head on the book, and when I look up Amir is there. Unexpectedly. It's difficult to recognize him at first. He looks a little darker, slimmer, and a bit unfamiliar.

After kissing the kids, he tells them to go and play in the yard. I say, "No, stay here." They will make noise in the yard.

Being alone together is nothing like what happens in the movies. There is no sound, no music. Like a man and a woman who run into each other in the street, we are supposed to remember that we somehow know each other. But remembering alone is not enough. There is a need for something more, perhaps something that has to do with love. Amir comes close and touches my arm.

I say, "I'll get you some tea."

He follows me to the kitchen but doesn't let go of my hand. "I won't go back to Baku any more. I'll stay right here."

47

Maman says, "Promise you won't tell anybody."

Shahla is opening canned fruit for Maman.

"I want everybody to look at my face when I am talking."

I laugh, "At your nose?"

Moaning, she says, "Yes, but not at my breasts."

I stare at her face to avoid looking at her chest. Her face looks old.

"It's my bad luck that the surgeon did such an awful job. The chest should feel smooth, even with no breast. These scars upset me. The skin should be soft, like normal skin."

My heels are itching. So are my fingertips.

Shahla goes out to shop.

"But it's not smooth. Sometimes I go crazy and want to put a hot iron on my chest and smooth it out." Maman moans.

"Are you in pain?"

I am waiting for her to show me where it hurts. I point to her chest.

She says, "No."

Her hand is searching for pain in the air. She doesn't know the exact place it hurts. Perhaps she is in no pain at all. She moans louder as if reading my mind. I know this weeping.

I am used to it like an old nanny. It's old. Her chest is not smooth because of age. Her weeping is gloomy and hoarse.

But it's a lie. I have not gotten used to this noise. I don't like Maman's weeping. I am not happy. I know I am frowning and don't look anything like a cheerful and smiling nurse. Maman is unhappy too. Sickness hasn't given her the yielding and accepting face that makes one look calm.

"If Mahin were here, she would have thought of something."

I don't know what Mahin would have done that Shahla and I can't. The look of an impending crying fit covers her face. I bring her milk and straighten up her sheets. I arrange her medicine on a plate and repeat the order in which they should be taken. This is all because there is nothing else I can do. All patients need sympathy. And I am no good at expressing that.

48

I can't sympathize with Amir either.

"Although she didn't continue her education, her life was turned around. If she had stayed here, she would have been an ordinary and uneducated woman, like hundreds of others. But now . . ."

Amir is thinking about his friends, and with every sentence he looks at me. He is waiting for me to say something so he could talk more passionately about that other world. It's enough to say, "But her husband got sick; he was depressed."

Then he starts quietly and convincingly, "I know, they have their own problems too, but their issues are different."

Then his voice becomes louder little by little. "You don't understand what it means to find a finger behind the workshop. You don't understand what seeing a thirteen-year-old girl who is a drug addict and is willing to do anything for money, does to you."

Amir needs a nudge to pour out his heart. Silently, I go to the backyard. The sound of the tambourine has started, albeit late.

He says, "Shut that door. For one night don't listen to the orchestra. Come here and sit down."

I sit by him and ask, "Has something happened?"

I know that a breeze has stirred in his direction from another world, like the smell of barbecue that comes from far away and tickles your nose.

"What did you want to happen?" Gently, he puts his arm that is stiff like a wooden stick on his eyes. "You stay at home and have no idea what is happening out there. If you knew, you wouldn't say these things."

I don't know what I have said.

"You are willing to live in this awful and hideous place even if you were to relive it a hundred times over. Isn't that so?"

I want to scream "No," but I feel like a convict whose confession or silence wouldn't change her death sentence.

"Think about it. The kids will have good educational opportunities. They can use their talents. Nobody will put them down."

At least if he takes his arms off his eyes, he wouldn't look so much like somebody who is stuck under the rubble.

I get up and wash the dishes that are left from dinner. I shoo the mosquitoes out of the room and close the windows. Amir has fallen asleep with the story he has told himself. I pull a blanket over him and with my new obsession make sure the door and windows are locked. The air is cool, and here and there the windows of the houses across the street are lit. I put away Amir's toothbrush, straighten out the kids' covers, and take a second look at the kitchen. Everything is in its place; tidy and neat. I lie down only to realize that there is no use. There is no use shutting the doors and the windows. Insecurity has crept into the house like a filthy cat, and I know that even if I close my eyes, I'll hear its evil snore in my dream.

49

 I scream.

"Don't I have the right to have anything private for myself in this house?"

Amir is quiet. The back of his neck has turned red and that's a bad sign.

I holler again. Amir has read the letter that I wrote to Mahin, and is now waiting like a witness that the judge hasn't summoned in yet.

To get him to talk, I scream at him like a sharp needle against a pimple.

He says, "Now I understand why I never liked your mother."

I don't know if I should fight him for reading the letter or for what he is thinking about my mother. I say, "You had no right to read my letter."

"I had every right. Anything that concerns you in this house concerns me too."

There is no arguing about this point. It's an old argument that is repeated every now and then. I sometimes prefer privacy but he believes in sharing everything. I try hard to remember what I had written in my letter.

"She is being punished for it."

I look at him, surprised. "Punished for what?"

"Punished for her cruelty, for being coldhearted. Now, watch how she's going to die, a hundred times worse than that poor man."

He goes to the fridge and says, "The poor thing."

Again Amir has thrown a word into the air, and I have to find out who it belongs to. I repeat to myself, "Poor Maman, poor Amir, poor Father." Like a dress, I hurriedly try the word on every person. I wonder who looks best in this dress.

Suddenly I wonder, "What if it belongs to me?"

50

Shahla is talking about Maman's bad temper, and it'll take some time before she begins to talk about her sickness. I listen quietly and I am preoccupied. Wherever I go, I don't stop thinking, even when I am changing Maman's sheets, or when I take Shadi to school and bring her back, or when I witness Hosseini's bloodshot eyes. Amir throws one leg over the other, and then again switches his legs. He has no problem with his legs. He has a problem with silence. He starts talking. No ears catch his words. They simply swell up and fill the room.

I go to the room where Manijeh is sitting. She looks like a passenger who has lost her ticket. I bring her back with me to the room where Amir and Hosseini are sitting.

Amir is signaling me with his eyes to say something, but I have become too dumb to get his signal. He is forced to send a more obvious sign. "I'll show you."

When you lose it, pulling yourself back together is very difficult.

We have left Manijeh's house. The kids are walking ahead of us. I am walking a little behind Amir. Manijeh is watching from her window. I wave to her. Amir pretends that he doesn't see her. We have to walk to the main street to find a taxi. We start walking in the dark, and I get started on my task. Like a spider, I hastily weave a web around myself and move inside it. This web is stronger than anything. Amir starts talking, and I swiftly continue my work like a woman who weaves a vest even with her eyes closed, and tell myself silently, "Now, see if you can get me."

51

Shahla comes with her hands full. "Why are you sitting in the dark?"

We don't say anything. She turns on the light and Maman blinks rapidly. I believe Maman has only one light, and when it's off it gets dark everywhere. Shahla has one extra light. That's why even when she is weeping and in the middle of crying and sobbing, she can tell the young girl who is standing nearby, "Mrs. So-and-So doesn't have tea," or ask her to bring tissue paper, or fill up the sugar bowl. Amir also has many lights. When the ones inside the house are off, he can turn on his own lights. That's why he can go to the swimming pool when we fight, or go for a big breakfast of tripe, or treat himself to a cool fruit juice and take off with his friends for the mountains.

Like Maman, I have only one light. When it goes off, it feels pitch black inside me. When I am mad, I am feuding with the whole world, and I am yet angrier at myself.

But Mahin has many lights. Her lights are constantly being turned on and off. It doesn't matter if a few of them are off. Some others are still on.

We gather around the packages that Mahin has sent. I open her letter, and Shahla opens one of the packages with a knife.

Mahin writes that she is now living with a wonderful young American. A picture of them is in the middle of a package of clothes. They have no problems. Only that sometimes they don't understand each other's language. Mahin hasn't written anything about her Iranian husband. Apparently, they lived together only for a few months. She writes about the lotions and the powders she has sent. I read a few lines while keeping an eye on Maman and Shahla, who have looked through the package and are now playing with a box that looks different.

Mahin says that this is the best quality imitation breasts she has found. She writes that they are a little small and are not as big as Maman's, which you could put a glass of tea on without worrying if it would fall.

Maman is lovingly cursing Mahin.

Shahla says, "Where did she find this long-legged guy?"

I take the picture and look at it. The long-legged guy is smiling. He looks biracial and is holding a happy Mahin under his wing like a tiny chick. The picture moves from hand to hand. The special box moves from hand to hand. The letter moves from hand to hand.

I have the picture again. I cover the body of the long-legged guy with my two fingers. I look at Mahin anew; frizzy black hair, naked arms, and tight shorts. I move the picture back and forth.

Maman looks at me with surprise, "Don't you recognize your own sister?"

52

I like the basement. Sometimes I like to go back there. Sometimes it's the only place that you can go from the ground level. It's been a long time since I realized that I have been carrying a basement within me. Since I have discovered the basement is my starting point, I stop there often. This time I have found the courage to walk there and carefully look at its walls. I have even considered putting up a light on the low ceiling. The basement no longer scares me. I want to go there. This time with my eyes open, feeling no fear.

I have been a tenant for thirty-five years in this basement, and now I have a sense of ownership. I want to find out about all its corners and passages. I want to see the stairs clearly, to get to know the hallways and look closely at the people. I have always looked at it through darkness and have seen only shadows and ghosts. How could I see anything else when fear blinded me and disgust stopped my breath?

Now I want to search all its gaps and openings in the light. The kids are calling me. The phone is ringing. Shadi puts a pencil sharpener in my hand, and I climb reluctantly out of the basement. I shake myself. I'm in no rush. I'm carrying out the kids' orders. I know that I can return to the basement anytime I want, like a traveler who returns to her homeland.

53

The woman enters the bedroom and the man, after apologizing, looks inside the room over the woman's shoulder. They apologize again for checking the bathroom. The real estate man winks at Amir. The sound of the tambourine is heard. The woman and man look at each other. The real estate man says, "What's that?"

He leaves, following the woman and the man. Amir follows them and returns after a few minutes.

The kids look at Amir as they watch me getting ready to leave. Amir is standing in front of the kitchen and looks like a warrior who can't believe his opponent is walking away quietly, leaving the battlefield.

I step outside. I am in the yard when Shadi taps on the window. From the movement of her lips, I realize she is asking for cheese puffs.

I start walking. I pass the intersection and go into a quiet alley. This alley has no resemblance to the other alleyways on this street. It has trees and smells nice, the scent of jasmine, the fragrance of roses, the aroma of freshly cooked rice. The houses have large windows and the chandeliers are visible through lace curtains.

"The person whose bird has already flown away has difficulty staying put. He'll become a stranger in his own house."

Do I have a bird too? My bird? But is it possible for anybody not to have a bird? Even the neighborhood gigolo,
with his dark glasses and curly hair, who is always lingering
in the streets, has his own bird. Whistling under his lips, he
is perhaps calling out for his bird.

Afterword

Fariba Vafi and Her Bird: On Pens and Feathers

FARZANEH MILANI

Pen and Feather are varieties of the same word, the root
being the Sanskrit *pat,* to fly.
    —Brewer, *Dictionary of Phrase and Fable,* 1894

In the cage of my breast / the birds of my words / have
lost their feathers.
    —Simin Behbahani, "In My Necessary Silence"

An unprecedented flourishing of women's literature—a
literary renaissance, really—is one of the collateral, unex-
pected benefits of the 1979 Islamic Revolution. Finally, the
pantheon of Persian literature is integrated in terms of the
gender of its producers, consumers, and objects of represen-
tation. Women are publishing a record number of books and
best sellers—fiction, nonfiction, poetry (exceptionally few of

I wish to express my gratitude to Kaveh Safa, who not only shares my
great enthusiasm for Fariba Vafi's work but also contributed with boundless
generosity of spirit and profound clarity of thought to this piece. I also want
to thank my good friend and colleague Rae Blumberg, who offered helpful
and astute comments, and my bright research assistant, Elizabeth Walsh.

133

which are available in the English language)—and winning some of the most prestigious literary awards. For the first time in Iranian history, a woman—Simin Behbahani—is Iran's national poet. Whereas there were a handful of women novelists before the 1960s, there are 370 of them now—thirteen times as many as ten years earlier and about equal to the number of men novelists.[1] Often women's novels outsell those of their male counterparts. While the average Iranian novel has a print run of about 5,000, several books by women have enjoyed printings of over 100,000 copies. The same phenomenal growth can be seen in the number of women working as literary translators. Whereas in 1997 Iran had 214 women translators, the number soared to 708 six years later. The number of women publishers almost doubled in that six-year period, rising from 66 to 103. Iran has the fastest-growing cyberspace and blogosphere usage in the Middle East, and here, too, women play a most active and defiant role.

The contribution of women to Iran's rich written literary tradition is nothing new. It can be traced back more than a thousand years to Rabe'e Qozdari, a tenth-century female poet writing at the very beginning of Persian literature. However, until the mid–nineteenth century, women's participation in published literature was sporadic and basically

1. These statistics are mainly taken from Hassan Mirabedini, "Dastan nevisiy-e zanan: gam hay-e larzan-e avaliy-e" [Women's Fiction Writing: First Wobbly Steps], *Zanan*, Mar. 2007, and Nazila Fathi, "Women Writing Novels Emerge as Stars in Iran," *New York Times*, June 29, 2005.

confined to poetry, which proved to be more woman-friendly than other public forms of art such as music, painting, sculpture, photography, or cinematography. Ali Akbar Moshir-Salimi, for instance, includes 294 women in his three-volume anthology about Iranian women writers from a thousand years ago published in 1956, and all 294 women are poets.[2] Moreover, for a variety of reasons—access to education and leisure and the two essential conditions for creativity that Virginia Woolf insisted on: a room of one's own and financial independence—writing, or at least publishing, was the prerogative of women of the court and high aristocracy.[3] Out of the 107 poets anthologized by Keshavarz Sadr in his book *Az Rabe'e ta Parvin*, published in 1956, 43 are members of the court and the rest belong almost exclusively to the upper class.[4]

Exceptions aside, for centuries the power and privilege of the written word belonged mainly to men. In a society concerned with keeping the worlds of men and women apart, with an ideal of femininity as enclosed, silent, and invisible, women writers could not easily flourish. They had to subvert a powerful system and negotiate rules of modesty

2. Ali Akbar Moshir-Salimi, *Zanan-e sokhanvar az yek hezar sal-e pish ta emruz* [Persian Women Writers from a Thousand Years Ago until Today] (Tehran: Elmi: 1956–58).

3. Virginia Woolf, *A Room of One's Own* (1929; reprint, New York: Harcourt, 1957).

4. Keshavarz-e Sadr, *Az Rabe'e ta Parvin* [From Rabe'e to Parvin] (Tehran: Kavian, 1956).

that not only minimized physical contact between the sexes, but also forbade free circulation of their bodies and their voices in open spaces. It is only in the mid–nineteenth century that more and more women appeared in public places and demanded expansion of their citizenship rights. Women writers, always at the forefront of sociopolitical movements in Iran, broke the spell of their textual quasi invisibility by entering public and discursive spaces. They were no longer isolated exceptions. There were finally a considerable number of authors and texts and an uninterrupted chain of literary foremothers.

Today, more than three decades after the Islamic Revolution and in spite of all the problems—social and economic hardships, censorship, the need to conform to Islamic morality, the eight-year war with Iraq, incarceration, cancellation of permits to print—or perhaps because of them, a larger and more diverse group of women has appeared on the literary scene, enjoying the kind of fame and popularity reserved hitherto for male writers. Religious and secular, westernized and traditional, highly educated and holders of high school diplomas, upper-, middle-, and lower-class women write from a variety of perspectives and enrich the literary discourse. Women's issues are no longer considered solely the concerns of elite women, personal, private, or unavoidable. They are presented as gendered inequities, endemic to an entire social structure that can and ought to be changed.

Fariba Vafi, whose most highly acclaimed book is translated here for the first time, is one of the leading voices in this vibrant scene.[5] She was born in the city of Tabriz, 335 miles northwest of Tehran, on January 21, 1962. Unlike the majority of women writers who are from the capital city and belong to well-educated and elite families, she grew up in a provincial capital where Azari Turkish is the spoken language, attended public school there, and underwent a traditional upbringing in a family she characterizes as not highly educated. Soon after graduation from high school, she began working in a plant that manufactured women's clothing, and later worked in a nursery school in order to be economically independent and able to buy books.[6] Leaving both jobs, she spent a year in a police training school in Tehran, which became the inspiration for her second novel, a book titled after its main protagonist, *Tarlan.*[7] Upon her return to Tabriz, she served as a warden in the Women's Prison, where she lasted only three months.

When she was twenty-six, Vafi married Majid Rahbar-e Azadi. Her first child, a son named Elshan, was born a year later in 1990, followed four years later by a girl, Elyar. Although "[m]arriage and children delayed her plan

5. *My Bird* is also being translated into Italian.

6. Personal communication, May 23, 2009.

7. As Nazila Fathi observes, in *Tarlan,* Vafi "describes women from poor families, who enter the harsh environment of the police school. The book arouses readers' sympathy for policewomen who must enforce the strict social code of Islam and who are widely resented in Iran for harassing women who deviate from Muslim dress rules," *New York Times,* June 29, 2005.

to become a novelist," as she told Nazila Fathi of the *New York Times*,[8] Vafi never relinquished the dream of becoming a writer. Unlike several influential women writers—Parvin E'tessami, Goli Taraqi, Simin Daneshvar, Simin Behbahani, Forugh Farrokhzad—she was neither related to nor connected with prominent writers. To seek comments by a professional writer, she found the home address of Jamal Mir-Sadeqi (1933–), a prolific writer and teacher of fiction.[9] One day after the publication of her first collection of short stories, she knocked on his door with samples of her writing. With tenacity and resolve, she traveled by bus to Tehran every other month, accompanied by her children, to show him her work.

Vafi entered the literary scene in 1988 with a short story, "You're at Peace Now, Father," published in the journal *Adineh*.[10] Although she continued to publish her short stories in literary journals such as *Doniya-ye Sokhan* and *Chista*, it took her eight years to publish her first book, a collection of short stories titled *Dar Omq-e-sahneh* (In the Depth of the Stage,

8. Nazila Fathi, *New York Times*, June 29, 2005.

9. For a biographical sketch of Jamal Mir-Sadeqi and a translation of one of his short stories, "Through the Veil of Fog," see *Stories From Iran: A Chicago Anthology 1921–1991*, ed. Heshmat Moayyed (Washington, D.C.: Mage, 1991), 202–19. Mir-Sadeqi is the author of *Narrative Literature, the Tale, the Short Story, the Novel: A Look at Contemporary Fiction Writing in Iran*, among several other books.

10. "Rahat shodi pedar" [You're at Peace Now, Father] also appears in *Dar Omq-e-sahneh* [In the Depth of the Stage] (Tehran: Cheshmeh, 1996), 14–19.

1996).[11] In an outburst of creativity since then, she has published two other short-story collections—*Hatta vaqti mikhandim* (Even When We Laugh, 1999) and *Dar rah-e villa* (On the Way to the Villa, 2008)—plus four novels: *Parandehye man* (My Bird, 2003); *Tarlan* (2004); *Rowyay-e-tabbat* (Dream of Tibet, 2005); and *Razi dar kucheha* (A Secret in the Alleys, 2008).[12] Currently, she lives with her family in Tehran and is working on a new novel and a book for children and young adults, titled *Stories from Parvin E'tessami*. The latter is a prose rendition of forty poems by E'tessami, a pioneering woman poet celebrated for her versified stories.[13]

11. Vafi's short stories, which are often between four and seven pages long in the original Persian, have been called "sudden fiction" or "flash fiction." Perhaps the increasingly hurried impatience of life compels the skilled short-story writer to offer her tales in finite, quick bursts.

12. Few of Vafi's short stories have been translated into English. For "The Flight of the Sun," see Franklin Lewis and Farzin Yazdanfar, *In a Voice of Their Own* (Costa Mesa, Calif.: Mazda, 1996). For "My Mother Behind the Glass," see *A Feast in the Mirror: Stories by Contemporary Iranian Women*, ed. and trans. Mohammad Mehdi Khorami and Shouleh Vatanabadi (Boulder: Lynne Rienner, 2000), 201–5. "My Mother Behind the Glass" is also translated in *Afsaneh: Short Stories by Iranian Women*, ed. and trans. Kaveh Basmenji (London: Saqi, 2005), 172–76. For "On the Way to the Villa," trans. Yassaman Assa, see Iran's Literature Today: Glimmer in the Mist, www.iransliterature.com/page.asp?16.

13. *Stories from Parvin E'tessami* is part of a collection entitled *The Rereading of Ancient Books for Children*, which contains thirty books from thirteen classic Iranian authors and poets. "Author Vafi narrates E'tessami's poems for children," *Tehran Times*, May 20, 2009. V. 10595.

Vafi's first novel, *My Bird*, took the Iranian literary scene by surprise. It won a number of prestigious literary awards, including the Yalda Literary Prize, the Esfahan Prize, and the Golshiri Prize, and was chosen as Iran's best novel of the year in 2003. Containing fifty-three short, relatively self-contained chapters, the novel reads like poetry. The author, a master of verbal economy, weaves magic with words and creates her own signature style—minimalist, dazzling in its candor and courage, attentive to the smallest details, textured, empathetic, simple and revelatory, elegant and profound. She offers competing visions of truth, avoids judgment and absolutist pronouncements, and shows that the line between the victims and the victimizers is razor-thin.

Set in postrevolutionary Tehran, and all the more poignant for its condensed brevity (141 pages in Persian), *My Bird* is the lightly plotted coming-of-age story of a writer. It is the first-person narrative of a nameless thirty-five-year-old woman who lives with her husband and two children and shares certain biographical details with the author. Although originally the narrator resents being the sole caretaker of her two children, eventually she comes to view motherhood neither as stifling nor as her sole mission in life. She neither begrudges her maternal responsibilities nor does she romanticize motherhood.

The novel focuses on the search for and the emergence of an individual female self and on the liberating potential of storytelling. Its narrator vows to explore her life, her feelings, and her surroundings more carefully, and to describe them as accurately as she can. Reconstructing and reinscribing her subjectivity, she inches her way out of alienation and isolation and moves from an existential crisis to self-awareness and self-revelation. All the silence and secrecy and fear, all the scenes repressed but not forgotten, all the feelings buried but not dead that she carried around like the "hump" (10) of a hunchback, come unglued over the course of the novel. Like a freed bird, they fly out of the cage of their captivity.

The narrator of *My Bird*, like Edna Pontellier, the protagonist of Kate Chopin's *Awakening*, a canonical American text, is a woman who examines her place in society and escapes her gendered confinement. Although a devoted and compassionate wife and mother, she awakens gradually to the truth that she does not want to be restricted by traditional definitions of femininity. "I was sick and tired of my assigned role" (20), she writes. "I am not a mother, not a daughter, and not a wife. . . . I cannot perform any of the roles that have been assigned to me" (70), she laments. She feels bored, "bored of constantly having to take care of the kids, of the peeling walls, the broken water heater, the cockroaches that do not die with any kind of bug killer. She is tired of the long days turning to night, and of long nights that are filled with tears" (70). Married to a man, Amir, who often is away on business, and when home feels "chained" (40), or like "a migrant bird," who "is trapped in a cage," yearns "to fly" (68), she realizes she has "no place to go" (86). Even when she contemplates cheating on her quasi-absent husband, her imaginary betrayal is related to space and the suspension of her restrained physical mobility. "He doesn't know that I cheat on him a hundred times a day," she concedes. "I leave this life a hundred times a day. Like a terrified woman who has never left home. Gently, slowly, and quietly, even though scared to death, I secretly go to places that Amir cannot even imagine" (35). And so it is that she develops fantasies of flight and promises herself to define herself on her own terms and to "never again be dependent" (87), never again to be captive of an image or a role foisted upon her.

The promise the narrator of *My Bird* makes to herself is similar to Edna's. The strategies and tactics the two women adopt to establish their subjective identities, however, vastly differ. While Edna takes refuge in the welcoming sea and has to rely on the pen of Kate Chopin to memorialize her despair and defiance, the narrator of *My Bird* seeks and finds salvation in the act of writing. She takes up the pen, confronts the truth of her life head on, and throws away "such nonsense like a shared life, the warm family unit, and other rubbish" (106). She begins to make up her own definitions and to reimagine and rebuild her relationships. She undergoes two major and interrelated transformations. She breaks out of the physical confinement that impedes her freedom of movement and abandons the silence that constrains her freedom of expression.

Although Vafi, a voracious reader, does not recall ever reading *The Awakening*, the main character of one of her earliest short stories, titled suggestively "A Woman on the Shore," from her first published book, *In the Depth of the Stage*, eerily resembles Edna. When readers first meet the nameless protagonist of "A Woman on the Shore," she is taking care of her child, while her husband is joyfully swimming. Beckoned by the sea, mesmerized by its whispering voice, its magic and mystery, its majestic vastness, "the woman gets up with agility, rolls up her pants, and puts her feet on the warm, wet sand. A little wave embraces her feet and darts away quickly. Her naked feet follow the retreating wave."[14] The euphoric plunge, however, is short lived, at least for now. The sight of her child approaching the water makes the mother in her return to the shore. But "the desire to swim to the heart of the sea does not leave her alone." At long last, upon her husband's return, the woman hands him the child and "slides like a fish in the bosom of the waves." She does stop at one point to look at her family, but caressed by the seductive waves, she quickly decides to turn her back to the beach. "A feeling of joy forced her to run and to surrender her whole body all at once to the sea."[15]

14. Fariba Vafi, "A Woman on the Shore," *Dar Omq-e-sahneh* [In the Depth of the Stage], 84–87.

15. In one of the most anthologized poems of modern Persian literature, "O, People," Nima Yushij depicts the scene of a drowning man. His concern, however, revolves mainly around the complicity of all those uninvolved, carefree, and disengaged people who sit—"cheerful and laughing"—on the shore, witness the death of a struggling man "in the rough and formidable sea," and refuse to offer a helping hand to save him. The anguished voice of the poet and that of the drowning man mingle with the wind and the enveloping, angry waves and remind the reader of

Whether the woman's sensuous embrace of the sea is a triumphant liberation on dancing waves, an act of rebellion, a defiant refusal to be sucked in by motherhood, or a self-authorized death we will never know. A multiplicity of persuasive interpretations and closures is both valid and viable. Within the context of Vafi's whole body of work, however, it is safe to propose that the drowning protagonist serves as a warning to the author. The woman on the shore disappears in the roaring waves without redefining or articulating herself. Her voice is thus trapped, silenced, swept away. Literally and literarily, it is buried alive. Forewarned, the narrator of *My Bird* starts out where the woman on the shore ends up. She rejects her earlier silent expressions of captivity and rebellion, refuses the fate of numerous other defiant but drowning literary antecedents (Ophelia, Maggie Tulliver, Edna, and the woman on the shore, among many others), and stubbornly claims her right to live an independent life and express herself freely. Like a flying bird, she bursts into open space and begins to sing.

That is why bird symbolism is so central to the unfolding plot of Vafi's novel. For over one thousand years, free-roaming birds have epitomized for Iranian writers the liberty

---

an avoidable and cruel death. In his growing distress, the drowning man "raises above the water / now his head / now his feet / he has his eye on this world / and is shouting for help: / 'O, people!'" Nima Yushij, *Majmou'e-ye Ash'ar-e Nima Yushij* [Nima Yushij's Poetry Collection] (1955; reprint, Tehran: Safi Alishah, 1968), 178.

to wander at will, while their language, not tied to man-made rules, eloquent and universal, has stood for the song of a soul in its eternal search for identity, for voice and wing. *My Bird* begins and ends with references to birds. The story opens with a verbal map of the narrator's new neighborhood. In the cacophony of sounds and smells, in the landscape of smoky rooftops, small balconies, latticed iron doors, and cramped sidewalks where roses and jasmines are so "dusty" they cannot inspire poets and passersby—in this claustrophobic cosmos crowded with people, birds are a continuing inspiration and presence. "The third-floor neighbor keeps parrots," remarks the narrator in the first few lines of the book. "We also have a bird store down the street," she adds promptly. Birds appear and reappear throughout the novel and show up five times in as many lines in the last paragraph of the last chapter, bringing the book to a close. "Do I have a bird, too? My bird? But is it possible for anybody not to have a bird?" (131) asks the narrator rhetorically.

Harangued by a nagging sense of entrapment, the narrator goes looking for her bird. And this is quite an accomplishment for a woman who is associated throughout the novel not with birds, but with a zoo populated by heavy animals—polar bears, camels, crocodiles, buffalos, boars. At times, Amir calls her a "polar bear" (30; 52) because she does not participate in his restless and utopian fantasies of escape to Canada, because she fully understands the difference between forced mobility and the freedom of movement, because in his view she likes "to stay put," because she is "afraid of change . . . afraid of moving" (30). At other times, when he has had enough of her, her legs remind him of a camel (52). Sometimes, he sees her transformed "into a crocodile" (52), or "really fat, like a buffalo" (101). When the narrator's daughter gets mad at her, she draws her "with two big horns" on her head "and big teeth like a boar" (39). To reject all these unwanted analogies, the narrator gently strokes her own arm. "It's silky and smooth," she says with a sense of relief. "My hand should remain on my arm to feel its softness," she advises herself. "If I remove my hand, I might think I have the skin of a rhinoceros, the thick skin of a rhinoceros that would mistake hitting for caressing" (101).

Homebound rather than roaming freely, compared to nonflying creatures, the narrator looks for her bird. Refusing to be trapped by old and familiar cages, declining to whisper in the dark or to keep silent, she portrays the flying bird as a symbol of her sense of entrapment as well as her desire to take full flight and sing. Looking for her bird thus becomes synonymous with looking for her identity. Immobility of body and voice will no longer mark her thereafter.

The narrator is admired frequently for her silence. "I have been praised for it time and again," she confides. "I was seven or eight years old when I realized not all children have this virtue. My silence was considered my best asset" (19). Once when she refuses to answer her father's probing question regarding Aunt Mahboub, "not out of wisdom but out of fear," she realizes that her "simple and cowardly act of going mute" is turned into "a meaningful and wise silence" (20).

The positive reinforcement continues. "In later years, I was repeatedly admired by the women in the family for being reserved, for being secretive" (20). On rare occasions, when she abandons fleetingly her distinctive and celebrated quality, she earns the censure of her family and the epithet "tattletale." "I don't like tattletales," says a furious Aunt Mahboub. "She pressed her hand on my bony chest: 'A woman should learn to keep everything here. Do you understand?' I understood" (28). Although the narrator comes to the realization that just as "There are a hundred types of kindness" (17), there are also different varieties of silence, even though she knows all too well that full transparency is an illusion that refuses to be called what it is, she nonetheless vows to express the previously unarticulated.

If during her childhood the narrator was characterized above all by her silence, which was neither willed nor voluntary, if her silence had a "history" and was imposed on her through a complex system of reward and punishment, if she was like "a chest full of secrets with a tight lid" (20), she pledges to begin expressing the deepest emotions, naming forbidden feelings, uttering suppressed voices.[16] If she was

16. The narrator is horrified by the prospect that her daughter might turn into a windup doll, a vessel filled with silence or prerehearsed responses in delineated spaces. She does not want her daughter to take after her. "She has gone mute. A muffled sound comes out of her mouth. I see the fear in her eyes. I recognize silent crying very well. Silent crying means that she cannot leave" (39). Recognizing silent crying well, not wanting her daughter to be like her, she adopts a new strategy. "I sit Shadi

scared to go deep into the utmost reaches of her memory and her past—what she calls euphemistically "the basement"—she now wants to find the "courage to walk" there, "carefully look at its walls," and find out about all its "corners and passages," feeling "no fear" (129). She wants to turn her observing eye into a shining light and look through its darkness. In short, she wants to be able "to return to the basement" anytime she wants, "like a traveler who returns to her homeland" (129).

Although the narrator's change of consciousness happens in increments, the moment she deliberately travels to the basement and discards her mantle of silence and secrecy, which had bothered her "like a tight woolen dress in hot weather" (22), is such a turning point in her life that she

---

in front of me and give her a little lecture—what Maman should have done with me and never did. If I wanted to say something, I would pace up and down the room seven or eight times. I felt my heart in my throat and could not talk because it seemed like my words were stuck at the bottom of a deep well" (17). To teach her daughter a lesson, to extricate her voice from the bottom of that deep well, she grabs her doll, takes its battery out, and squeezes it. "'See,'" she tells her, "'if you don't make a sound, you are as bad as a doll without a battery, without a heart. Then it is possible to hurt you because nobody will even find out'" (18). Forugh Farrokhzad, too, was appalled by the possibility of becoming a windup doll and to "see the world through a pair of glassy eyes." Repulsed, she lamented: "one can sleep for years and years / in a velvet box / between layers of lace and tinsel / with a body stuffed with straw / With every squeeze of a shameless hand / one can declare / like a windup doll: / 'O, I am so very happy.'" Forugh Farrokhzad, *Tavalodi Digar* [Another Birth] (1964; reprint, Tehran: Morvarid, 1972), 71–75.

recalls it with precision and lucidity. "It was after Father's death that I broke my silence by screaming," she declares. "I wanted the whole world and everybody to know everything" (20). It is no accident that when the narrator of *My Bird* begins to write, and composes the critical letters to her sister, Mahin (chapter 25 and 45, both beginning with "I write"), she describes her repressed and painful recollection of Father's death. So, too, Fariba Vafi's first letter to the world—her first published short story, "You're at Peace Now, Father,"—revolves around and discloses the details of a painful memory, the death of the father in the basement.

Flying out of confinement and silence, the narrator breaks out of the cage of her former self. Celebrating her ability to speak her mind, she announces with great pride that "I write about me and the world around me" (110). Intoxicated from her sense of power and agency, believing in the transformative power of the pen, she thus moves from muteness to communication, from immobility to flight. Watching her creative energy kindled in front of her bedazzled eyes, she weaves words into a magic carpet, travels to forbidden territories, and beholds her imagination, which glides around "like a butterfly, showing off its wings that change color every second" (96). She converts her secrets and sorrows, the unwritten tale of her muted and concealed identity, the alienation written on her body, and the frustration scripted through her assigned roles into a novel. Her portable text cannot be chained, put behind bars, caged. Like a flying bird, it roams at will and goes to faraway places. It has just transmigrated, thanks to Mahnaz Kousha and Nasrin Jewell, to North America. The birth of the text, then, is a rebirth of the narrator. It frees her from the finiteness of her circumstances; it allows her to define for herself a new life as a woman: daughter, sister, wife, mother, and—no less important—as a writer as well. The nameless narrator grows wings, turns feathers into pens, allows her caged voice to soar, and becomes the highly acclaimed Fariba Vafi.

FARIBA VAFI was born in 1962 in Tabriz, Iran. She started to write short stories at a very young age. As a young girl, she frequently traveled to Tehran from her hometown of Tabriz, 335 miles away, to buy books and show her writing sketches to a literature teacher. Like most women writers throughout history, marriage and children delayed her plan to become a novelist. Starting to write in 1983, her fi rst short story collection, *In the Depth of the Stage (Dar Omgh-e-Sahneh)*, was published in 1986. The next short story collection, *Even While We Are Laughing (Hatta Vaqhti Mikhandidim)*, came out in 1999. She has written four novels: *My Bird (Parande-hye man)*, 2002; Tarlan, 2006; *Dream of Tibet (Rowyay-e-Tabbat)*, 2007; and A Secret in the Alleys (Razi dar Kucheha), 2008. She is currently working on the novel On the Way to the Villa (Dar Rah-e-vila). She lives in Tehran with her husband and two children.

NASRIN JEWELL is professor of economics at St. Catherine University in Saint Paul, Minnesota. Her current research area is redefining and reevaluating work, specifi cally applied to women in Iran. She has authored and collaborated on a number of articles on the role of women in economic development, the global economy and the New World Order, and women and work. She has been a Fulbright scholar to Caracas, Venezuela, and was a Midwestern Universities Consortium scholar in Madrid, Spain. Professor Jewell is a member of the board of directors of *Critique: Critical Middle Eastern Studies.*

MAHNAZ KOUSHA was professor of sociology at Macalester College, Saint Paul, Minnesota. Her book *Voices from Iran: Changing Lives of Iranian Women* (Syracuse University Press, 2002) explores family dynamics in Iran. She also conducted collaborative research on life satisfaction and happiness in Iran. Her areas of interest were race, gender, class, and family relationships in the United States and the Middle East.